The Saxon Ponds

The Saxon Ponds

THE SAXON PONDS

An Ancient Fishery Re-born

The Saxon Ponds

First published 2023 by Kindle Direct Publishing

Design by Peter Rolfe

Text ©Peter Rolfe

To my Civil Partner and fellow writer

Pam Kelly

and to my daughters

Teresa and Nicola

In memory of Mary

Other Books by Peter Rolfe

The Net on the Garage Wall: Medlar Press 1997, illustrated by S. Cork
Crock of Gold, Seeking the Crucian Carp: Mpress 2010
Reflections on Still Water, the Story of a Fishery: Mpress 2015
Always Summer: Medlar Press 2018, with Michael Pickford
One Last Cast: Mpress 2019, illustrated by Trevor Harrop
'The Trent Otter', J.W.Martin: Medlar Press 2021
Learning to Teach, 1955 – 2021: Peter Rolfe/Amazon 2022
The Net on the Garage Wall, 2nd Edition: Peter Rolfe/Amazon 2022
Happy to Take Risks: Peter Rolfe/Amazon 2022, with Pam Kelly
'The Trent Otter' – Man of Many Rivers: Peter Rolfe/Amazon 2023
Content with Small Pleasures – A Memoir: Peter Rolfe/Amazon 2023

THE SAXON PONDS

An Ancient Fishery Re-born

by

Peter Rolfe

The Saxon Ponds

The Saxon Ponds

Contents

INTRODUCTION
Page 9
PROLOGUE: Thinking of the Past
Page 11
CHAPTER ONE: Harvesting the Fish – Early Spring, 980 AD
Page 13
INTERLUDE
Page 25
CHAPTER TWO: 1895
Page 29
INTERLUDE
Page 41
CHAPTER THREE: March 1975 – 1992
Page 43
INTERLUDE
Page 57
CHAPTER FOUR: Extracts from a Notebook and the Random Thoughts of an Amateur Fishery Manager, 1992 – 2010
Page 59
INTERLUDE
Page 73
CHAPTER FIVE: The 'Dabblers' through the Years, 2011 – Nearly Now
Page 77
EPILOGUE: The Future
Page 127

The Saxon Ponds

The Saxon Ponds

Introduction

I have known the Saxon Ponds for just about 50 years and for 40 of those I have been actively involved in their management, for wildlife and for angling. They are small, something over half an acre each, situated on an unnamed brook that is a tributary of a famous river.

The ponds as I have known them are Victorian, but legend has it that they were there in the time of King Alfred, hence my name for them. Changes are now afoot. A new owner is re-landscaping the grounds of the big house and the lower pond has been changed and deepened. The upper pond awaits attention.

My involvement with this special place must shortly come to an end. Before that happens, I want to record the many years of my stewardship. Those years have been just one small part of the ponds' history.

What I have written is based upon imagination, research and my own journals, kept religiously over the 50 years. Just as important have been the extracts from my crucian website, written by some of the many who have fished the ponds and helped to maintain them.

That website would not exist but for the knowledge and dedication of one Cole Falconer, whose idea it was. I thank him for his technological brilliance, and for his support and friendship over many years.

I also want to thank Blanche Miller, the owner of the ponds until recent times, for her faith in my ability to look after them. Our partnership in that project was always amiable and based on mutual respect and cooperation. Had it not been for her and her brother's support when the ponds changed hands, my years of management would have come to an end much sooner. I should have regretted that.

The Saxon Ponds

   Last, my thanks go to the many anglers who have enjoyed the ponds and have helped me to maintain them. Their enjoyment of this special place is obvious from their contributions to the website, some of which are in Chapter Five. I have valued highly their cheerful hard work and their convivial company, but most of all their appreciation of the place itself.
   As I write this, things are changing at the ponds and it is not yet clear what will happen to the fishing once I retire. One thing is certain, that the ponds themselves will continue to be a haven for wildlife and for those who love quiet places. The new owner's concern for the ponds' environment assures me that they are in safe hands.

***

The illustrations come from several sources. Most are by Trevor Harrop and were originally done for *One Last Cast* in 2019. Trevor's fine work can be viewed at www.avondalegallery.com. The committee table at the head of Chapter Three was drawn by Stella Cork for the first edition of *The Net on the Garage Wall* in 1997. The front cover photograph is courtesy of Jim Wreglesworth. The others are freely available on the internet or from purchased prints.

The Saxon Ponds

PROLOGUE

Thinking of the Past

*I*t was a fine, dry March day and I was cutting back a willow by a favourite pond, one that I have known now for nearly 50 years. The 'chock' of billhook on timber and the rasp of the bowsaw filled the quiet valley, echoed from the façade of the handsome house and sent woodpigeons clattering aloft in the hazel wood on the hill, where it is said there was once a Roman road, now hidden by trees and bluebells.

It was a job I have done countless times and I was on autopilot, musing as I worked. I thought about how King Alfred's daughter, Aethelgifu, Abbess in the nearby hilltop town, was said to have eaten her Friday fish raised in the dark water of this pond and the one upstream, hidden from my view by a screen of trees.

There was no sign of such ancient occupation when, in the early 1970s, our yellow-cabbed excavator dug deep through sticky silt to hard, clean gravel. The only signs of the past we found then were the Victorian stone sluices, the brick-revetted island and a few marble-stopped bottles, dumped a hundred years ago in the wilderness of grass and nettles.

Remembering this, I wondered just how many times over the centuries the tiny stream that fed the ponds had filled them with mud, so that water became bog; how many times had labourers sweated there with basket, cart and shovel, to bring cool clearness back, for insects, birds, for fish, and water-spellbound folk like me.

Later, in front of my computer, I began to weave a story through time, based on the few facts I could discover. This is that story.

The Saxon Ponds

The Saxon Ponds

CHAPTER ONE

HARVESTING THE FISH

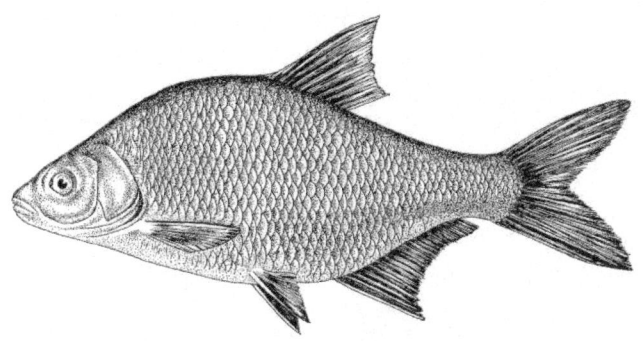

Early spring 980 AD

Rolf was a 'thicke knarr', like Chaucer's Miller, tall amongst his fellows, broad-shouldered, strongly muscled and rough-bearded, about 29 years of age, in his full maturity. With luck he would live to the ripe old age of 40. Whether he could have heaved a door off its hinges by butting it at a run is a different matter, but he was certainly not a man to trifle with. Strong of body, resourceful and intelligent, he was well-fitted for his job, fish master for the Abbess Herleva.

On that fine dry March day, he was a happy man. It had been a good day's work. He gave a grunt of satisfaction as he watched the last cowle of fish carried across the earth dam of the upper pond, slung from a pole carried by Gurt and Tam. There were many big tench and eels, some as big as two pounds, to be carted up the hill to Sceptesberie and stocked into the Abbey stew ponds. The Abbess

The Saxon Ponds

and her nuns would have plenty of fresh fish for special feasting in the year ahead. Indeed, rumour had it that the Bishop of Salisbury and his retinue would be entertained by the abbess just after Easter. A fine banquet would be prepared, with a roast swan as the centrepiece on the long oak table, with fine silver tableware and tall drinking cups, just as Rolf remembered from many years ago when, as a boy, he had served the Abbess and her guests in the great hall.

He and his men had been ready at cock crow to gather the last of the fish. For two days before this, as the sluice boards were lifted and the water level fell a hand's breadth every four hours, they had dragged the heavy nettle hemp net through the pond, catching mostly the bream, deep-sided like meat platters. The tench and eels, though, were more difficult. They lurked in the mud at the bottom of the pond and almost all avoided the net. More leads on the bottom of the net might have kept the net down enough to capture them, but the bottom silt would have held back the net and made everything much heavier and exhausting. Rolf preferred to do things his way.

Even so it had been demanding work. Once all the water had gone downstream, red-haired Tam, old man Edmund and he had waded in the shallow water and shin-deep mud, scooping the fish into willow baskets. Dragged to the bank, the baskets were then emptied by stalwart Gurt into a barrel of water to clean the fish of mud, thence to the cart in the carrying baskets filled with wet reeds. Tench and bream and eels travelled well in that way, hardy fish indeed in the cool of the year, and the skips were lighter than water-filled barrels.

The two oxen would be glad of that by the time they had climbed the last slope. He heard one snort, as if in agreement, the sound brought to him by the stiff southerly breeze as the cart began its journey, lurching up the rutted track that led eventually to Sceptesberie, some four miles away, with his men clinging on and steadying the load. Once there, the fish would be tipped into the Abbey stew ponds until their time came to be eaten. Rolf waved farewell and Edmund waved back.

The Saxon Ponds

Only those fish big enough to eat made the journey, as always. The smaller ones had been moved to the lower pond to grow bigger. Next year it would be the turn of that pond to be netted. And so, the cycle continued, year in, year out, with each pond drained and dried every third or fourth year. Rolf had learned many of his skills from his work as a younger man on the Abbey ponds on the side of Sceptesberie Hill but in fish management he was ahead of his time. He believed that to leave a pond dry and fallow to sweeten and regain its energy every third or fourth year led to a bigger, healthier crop, though others might scoff at the idea.

Rolf himself could not abide the taste of fish, much preferring hare or roedeer, which were plentiful in the valley and could be trapped and hunted. He had heard that pickerel and perch were tastier than bream or tench, but he knew that they ate other fish, and the Abbey ponds were too small to support such greedy creatures. He would often shrug his shoulders when someone asked him if he ate the fish he caught. No doubt some folk preferred any sort of fresh fish to the smoked or salted herrings and mackerel that the nuns usually ate on non-meat days, but he did not have to do the same.

He turned to go into the cottage, muscles suddenly aching from the arduous work. Getting old, he thought. The fish house stood on a level piece of ground to the south of the two ponds. It was thatched with wheat straw and built of the timber from the edge of Berrywood Forest, dark and mysterious on the high land opposite, occupying the landscape as far as the eye could see to the north of where he stood.

Rolf was not one to fear much, but Berrywood Forest was old beyond memory, dark and wild, and he would not enter it. He kept to his watery and reedy domain, where the sun shone and the sky was open. It was said that a witch lived in her hovel on the other side of the forest and that children had disappeared from the village in the past. It was said too that there was an ages-old road through the forest, haunted by Roman legionaries, and though part of him

The Saxon Ponds

scoffed at the idea, another side of him half believed such tales, like the one about a great Druid oak where hooded figures performed their mysterious rites and sacrificed human victims.

It was trackless. Once lost there, you would never find your way out. There were fierce animals, too; dangerous wolves and wild boar that roamed freely. Some men did venture there, though. As he looked up the hill, he saw the thin spires of smoke curling upwards from the charcoal burners' kilns. Strange and mysterious people they were, to be sure, shunned by normal, God-fearing folk. He impulsively crossed himself.

With an effort, he climbed the ladder to his living quarters. The ground floor was where he kept his nets and traps and the other paraphernalia of his trade. The smell of fish seeped up into the room above, but Rolf had long since ceased to be aware of it; long exposure had dulled his senses.

His home was rough and ready, though it suited him well enough – there were plenty who had to make do with worse. The light was fading and the trestle bed looked welcoming, with its straw palliasse and sheepskin cover, but first he eased himself on to a homemade stool and sat at the makeshift table for some refreshment, cold meat from the hare he had snared three days ago and had cooked on a spit over the open fire, a chunk of bread made from wheat and rye by Old Meg in the village, washed down with strong beer from the small barrel in the corner of the suddenly darkening room. The fire had long gone out, though the room still smelled of smoke and there was just a smidgin of heat in the embers, but it was too late to light it again. Sleep beckoned.

That night he slept the sleep of the just. Tomorrow, he would need to visit the village for stores and barter for bread and beer with the promise of fish in return, but the thought did not keep him awake for long. Nor did the shrieks of the white owl who lived in the hollow oak by the lower pond, nor the caterwauling of Grimalkin and the others from the storeroom below, where they kept vermin from the nets and baskets. Perhaps a tom cat had come visiting from the

The Saxon Ponds

village; perhaps later there would be kittens to drown in a weighted sack. Those were his last thoughts as he settled his head on the rough pillow. His snores reverberated round the small room but there was no-one to be disturbed by them. His dreams were of water, mud and fish, and of a job well done.

***

He awoke with the lark, as the first rays of the sun reached the ponds. The sound of small birds was everywhere. Spring was coming and there were territories to be claimed. Rolf grimaced as he levered himself out of bed, stiff from all the bending and lifting of yesterday.

From the slot of a window, he saw a wide-winged bird of prey circling the small area of grass on the hillside below the forest, searching for voles or young hares. Predatory birds were common enough in this valley overlooked by wild upland, buzzards, kites and windhovers particularly - one wild autumn day, he had seen a hunting family of five windhovers etched against the white cloud, a splendid sight. Red-tailed kites were always searching around his dwelling in the spring for stuff to make their nests, so that leaving linen on a bush to dry was asking to have it stolen by the bold birds. He admired their cheekiness and their fine plumage, even though they could be such a nuisance.

Sperhauks sometimes flashed through the trees after prey and a smaller hawk with swept-back wings often chased the horse-stingers in the summer sun. Once he had seen a white-tailed eagle and two or three times a fish hawk. In his father's day, he had been told, these giant birds were everywhere and their prey abundant. Hunting had diminished both, Rolf feared. The times were changing, and he regretted it.

He breakfasted on rough porridge oats and milk from his cow, which foraged the rough pasture behind the cottage. The milk tasted slightly sour – he had been too busy over the past few days to milk afresh. The lone calf had benefited to the full instead. More cold

The Saxon Ponds

meat, bread and ale finished his meal. He was ready for the day, to check the pond, dig and rake his vegetable patch ready for sowing, milk the cow, and visit the village if he had the time.

The cottage faced south, to catch the early-morning warmth of the sun, but Rolf breakfasted on the north side of the room, where, through the eye slots that brought some light into the dwelling, he could see both ponds. He watched carefully while he ate. A man who looked after the Abbess's ponds had to be suspicious and alert. Fish were valuable and it was his job to ensure that they stayed safe. He kept a cudgel by his trestle bed to defend against human intruders, and a sturdy bow leaned against the wall next to the leathern quiver of arrows.

There were more than human thieves to worry about. Herons and otters abounded in the valley, and he needed to keep a keen eye open for them. His traps and snares, and his hazelwood angle and horsehair line, - he smiled at the thought of them – were stored below with the nets.

By the ponds, he knew how to read the signs of creatures feeding on his fish. Piles of scales with bones amongst them meant that an otter had been on a rampage. Sometimes there would be sweet-smelling droppings on the sluice wall. Solid white smears on the bank, or a floating fish with a wound behind the head showed that Old Nog had been fishing. Sometimes a small fish would be floating, half dead from a damaged head, the work of a dive dapper, he supposed. Their wailing calls often made him shiver. 'Twas said they were the cries of imprisoned souls desperate to escape.

Today, though, there was no need to worry about security of the upper pond. It was empty of fish and water, save for a few shallow pools surrounded by mud. He smiled as he thought of how the tench had hidden in the liquid silt of such pools, and how he and his men had to lift out the slimy, slippery creatures by hand, groping in the mud until they felt the fish.

In the flat early light, a heron was standing near the top of the pond, looking intently at the puddle at his feet, with the same

The Saxon Ponds

hope. Alarmed by Rolf's opening the cottage door, it croaked aloft on its wide wings, letting fall a stream of whitewash, and Rolf cursed under his breath at a lost opportunity. His bow stood idle by the bed.

He wondered if birds somehow talked to each other, a sort of parliament of fowls. He saw bobbing sandpipers with their white undersides only when he had drained a pond, never at any other time. How did they know the pond was empty? Mire snipe, too, somehow always found the mud, coming and going in groups of three or four even while he stood there. He loved their eery drumming in the spring, so unlike the singing of other birds, their swooping flight and their sudden, zigzag escape when he disturbed them from their secret places. Already the mud was criss-crossed with their tracks and those of other birds, voles and mice. The mud was like a broad highway with countless pilgrims, most of them night visitors.

He checked the sluice with its neatly stacked boards already drying in the early spring sunshine before continuing round the pond, looking for fish that had been missed, to rescue and place in the other pond. Mussels had left winding trails in the mud where they had tried to find fresh water. At the end of each trail, there the mussel lay, frustrated in its quest, and Rolf gathered three for supper into the bucket he was carrying. He had never tried to eat them before and wondered how they could be best prepared. Otters enjoyed them, crows and rats too – so why not humans?

He gathered half a dozen small crabba, laughing aloud at their feeble attempts to nip his gnarled fingers, from where the brook entered the pond, lifting stones to find them. The water was cold and fresh, the sound of it refreshing. He knew how delicious these little, white-clawed creatures were, dropped into boiling water and turning pink and succulent. The mussels would do the same. Supper was catered for, with the last of the turnips and wild carrots from the clamp.

The Saxon Ponds

The brook had already begun to carve its channel through the soft mud, exposing the gravel beneath. It snaked its way down to the nearest pool and found its way down to the sluice.

This year, Rolf mused, there was no need to set the serfs to work with spades and baskets to dredge the mud, still shallow after the last draining. *We need some dry weather*, he thought, *way into the Easter month and beyond. May St Benedict serve us well!* Then the grass and the sweet flowers would grow in the empty pond for the sheep to graze over the summer. Their dung would enrich the mud, their hooves diminish the dry silt. *Then, let there be water enough to fill the pond again*. Next spring, small fish from the other pond would find rich feeding and would grow fast.

The brook that fed the ponds had no name. It emerged from the bogs that filled the valley for an unknown distance to the west. Rolf had once explored the approaches to this wet and treacherous area, where the reeds grew head-high and muddy pools threatened to engulf the unwary. He had once stumbled into deep mud and had struggled to escape. It was as if some force was determined to suck him down, grasping his legs, determined never to let him go. That had frightened him badly and he had never ventured there again.

He was used to the strange sounds of the bog: the deep, hollow booming of the bittern, the drumming snipe and the ghostly calling of the curlews. They did not frighten him as they would other men. There were other strange sounds that he had come to love, the weird calls of the wild geese and the wingbeats of the great white swans. But he sensed that behind these familiar sounds there were others that he could not quite hear, strive though he did, those of threatening other-worldly things in the great bog.

Who could really tell what lurked there? When the wind moaned through the willows, their limbs moving like strange living things in the half-light of dusk, it was easy to believe in the elf-king and his brood who would suck the soul from a man. Will-o'-the-wisps, too, that would lead him to a miserable death in the mire – Rolf himself had seen the sinister, moving glow of such a phantom

The Saxon Ponds

from his window. Perhaps the Green Man himself held court there, the god of superabundance in the spring. Rolf feared wizards and witches too. Deep in that mysterious region, anything might lurk.

Rolf turned to more comfortable things. In the brook at his feet, he saw a movement. Crabba? No. A small fish was digging a hole! What a wonder! He watched, fascinated, how it picked particles of gravel from the brook bed and dropped them downstream. Did fish build nests like birds, he thought. He wished he could see more closely what was happening, but the twists and turns of the current obscured his view. Another mystery to join so many others, like how some beetles glowed in the dark or caterpillars had children. And horse-stingers, so abundant when the sun shone, where did they go to in the rain? Where were swallows in the winter? Some said they went to sleep in hidden places, as hedgepigs and Brock did. But why did they flock so at the end of summer? And where did cuckoos build their nests? Rolf had never found one, though he had seen baby cuckoos in reed warbler nests, many times bigger than the other fledgelings.

Rolf was seldom lonely, though it was a solitary life he led. He had no wife to warm his bed, no children to play around his cottage – *thanks be to St Benedict,* he thought. Visitors were infrequent. An occasional walk over the river footbridge to the village for supplies was his social highlight or a rare evening at the tavern with Gurt and Tam and Edmund if he had half a coin to spend. For female company, there were willing dames enough in the village, though he craved their prattling company but seldom. His features were hinted at in the faces of three or four of the village children.

Winter days sometimes seemed long, and it was then, if ever, that company was more welcome and the walk to the village less burdensome. He was hardened to the cold and the valley was sheltered from all but the biting easterlies that came at the time of the blackthorn. He had the firewood that he had gathered and chopped at the end of summer stacked in a lean-to handy to the door of the cottage, and a good fireplace in the centre of the room.

The Saxon Ponds

He was cosy enough beside the fire's crackling, turning a hare on the spit.

Winter's wet weather he liked least and at such times he shivered bad-temperedly. The valley became a morass after a wet November and in a bad year his joints could suffer for weeks on end, but he welcomed the frost that hardened the ground and the snow that often lay thick on the iced-over ponds. In the wet times, he could console himself only with the thought that it was the rain that kept the springs flowing and his beloved ponds alive.

When the spring came, though, and the cuckoo's song echoed through the valley, with the nightingale still to come, winter's hardships were forgotten. Around him was a landscape of plenty; he felt no need then of fellow human beings. His enquiring mind made every day fulfilling. He could hunt and trap for his food and sometimes even angle for pleasure – just to find out how many fish were there and how they were growing, he told himself.

Sitting still by the water, sheltered by the alders, he found that the animals and birds came to him, and that gave him a strange pleasure. The waterhens fussed over their black dandelion seed chicks, wild duck led their brood across his line of view, swallows and martins swooped. He had seen wily Reynard carrying his prey, usually a hen from the village, wings still flapping, and heard Tommy Brock snort in the half-light. Flying mice, big and small, gyrated above his head at dusk. Banshee ules called in their ghostly way.

Rolf felt no urge to hunt and kill the creatures so abundantly around him, except to feed himself or to protect the Abbess's fish. His life was defined by the seasons and the movement of the sun. He rose at sunrise and went to his bed at dusk, unless the fishing kept him up a little later. The ponds he looked after and the creatures that lived in and around them were the centre of his life.

Sometimes he wished he could record the thoughts and feelings his narrow world inspired but he could neither read nor write. He would leave nothing behind him when his time came, beyond a brief memory or two in the minds of those who had known

The Saxon Ponds

him. Even those would soon die, and it would be as if he had never existed.

Eventually, after the Dissolution of the Monasteries, even the ponds that had been Rolf's care would disappear; they would fill with silt and become dry land. It would be many centuries before they held water again.

The Saxon Ponds

The Saxon Ponds

INTERLUDE

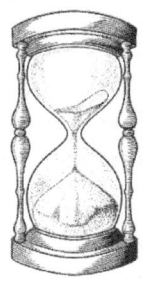

Historians tell us that in 1532, Henry the Eighth broke with the Church of Rome. From north to south, east to west, monasteries and abbeys were abandoned, Catholic priests, monks, friars and nuns absorbed into the population at large. This was the Reformation.

From 1539, the Abbey on the hill was left untenanted, except for ghosts and memories. For centuries it had been the wealthiest Benedictine Abbey in the country. At its peak, it had housed over 120 nuns. As the resting place of the bones of St Edward the Martyr, it had been renowned as a destination for devout and hopeful pilgrimage. Now it fell to ruin. The bitter upland winter winds whined through the broken stones. A glory had passed.

The ponds in the valley too were abandoned. Nature, as is her wont, quickly reclaimed them. Mud accumulated, water shallowed until first reeds, then willow and alder, grew where fish once swam. The great bog extended to occupy the ponds. Rolf's fish house, untenanted, crumbled, its timbers shrinking in the sun and rotting in the winter rains.

The Saxon Ponds

As the years turned to decades and the decades to centuries, man's hand played a greater part. The ancient forest was tamed and felled: it became a wood and then a coppice, where hazel was managed for hurdle-making. In the place of witches, druids and ghosts, a Puritan clergyman, Peter Ince, preached there to his open-air congregations.

By the nineteenth century, Rolf's hamlet had become a thriving village. There were mills on the river into which the erstwhile ponds had drained. The church was enlarged and modernised, the rectory assumed greater importance. There were carpenters, a mason, gardeners, a chimney sweep in Barker's Street, a horse breaker, carpenter and dressmaker who lived on Barkers Hill. Stone masons and a dress maker were in Pigs Trough Lane. A miller and dressmaker lived in Brick Yard. Mill Lane had a lot of brick makers, a grocer, two blacksmiths, a dressmaker, miller, innkeeper, tailor, shoemaker and a thatcher who was also the parish clerk. There was also a groom and a veterinary surgeon. The inhabitants of Scott's Hill were a brick labourer, a brick and tile maker and again, a dressmaker. South Hill had a carter and Hernshaw Street had two stone masons and a warrener. In Water Street there was a police constable, a grocer and shoemaker, a carter, gardener and a shepherd. There were also many agricultural labourers and a few farmers in the surrounding parish.

As for the forgotten ponds, there was just a local half-memory that an 18th century divine had tried to have them restored...but that was nothing more than legend. Fields grazed by sheep and cattle were in their place, with spinneys of willow, alder and damp-loving flowers in the wetter hollows.

Then, in 1875, one Horace Edward Chapman became the incumbent of the village church and moved into the rectory. When his Roman Catholic leanings and his love of High Church ceremony led to his resignation in 1891, he converted to his preferred religion, bought the rectory for his large family, and turned his mind to modernising it and landscaping his estate. He had married well, was

The Saxon Ponds

a wealthy man in his own right and spared no expense in his improvements to house and garden. The latter was extended and walled; fine lawns and a small orchard graced the scene; a trout-filled, clean and abundant brook chattered its way down its valley and reminded Chapman that a country gentleman must have a lake, as all great houses had. That is where my story resumes.

The Saxon Ponds

The Saxon Ponds

CHAPTER TWO

1895

Horace Chapman, one time-vicar of the parish church of St Andrew and wealthy landowner on the edge of aristocracy, was sitting at his father's huge mahogany desk in the study of what had once been the rectory, poring over a heavy, brown leather-bound accounts book. A chessboard and chessmen, antique and finely crafted, the court figures those of Norse gods with tunicked dwarfs for pawns, was on the desk beside the book, the

The Saxon Ponds

game half played. Chess, for once, must play second fiddle to weightier matters.

As usual, he was concerned about money. He was a rich man who had succeeded to his father's estate just four years before but worry came naturally to him and he had spent lavishly since making the rectory his own property; he had extended and improved it, had built Beauchamp House as a replacement dwelling for the Protestant vicar who had usurped his place, as he saw it, and had landscaped his own fine grounds. In 1893, indeed, so worried had he been about his resources that he had spent time in Salisbury Asylum with nervous exhaustion. Could he possibly afford his next dream, an imposing estate lake as a backdrop to the walled garden and orchard?

There was a quiet knock at the study door and his wife Adelaide came in, her usual good-humoured expression tempered by curiosity. "Horace, there is a man to see you, a Mr Ralph? He says he's been sent by Mr Ford, all the way from Lincolnshire, and that you were expecting him?"

"Ah, the man who'll tell us whether the ground will suit our new fishpond." Horace looked askance at his wife's bemused expression. "My dear... I'm sure I told you he was coming today."

His wife smiled, without answering. She was used to Horace's preoccupations and extravagant ideas, and his occasional failure to tell her about them. The maid ushered in the visitor, and after the usual pleasantries Adelaide left them to it. She must instruct Greaves the housekeeper to arrange an extra place at the lunch table. That duty done, the sound of her grandchildren playing took her mind away from domestic routine. She was a happy woman, who tried to count her blessings every day, and her family was foremost among those blessings.

Mr Ralph was knowledgeable, Horace had to admit, though his broad East Anglian accent took some understanding. The two of them spent an hour in the wild area to the west of the garden, an oddly assorted pair: Mr Ralph tall and lean, well over six feet, rugged

The Saxon Ponds

and tanned from his outdoor life; Horace, immaculately dressed in the new-trend plus-fours and hacking jacket, and portly from good living.

"There must've been ponds here in the past," speculated Mr Ralph, as they picked their way through the goat willows that grew thickly in the dell. Three giant alders towered above them.

"So tradition says, Mr Ralph. Talk has always been that this was part of the Abbess's land way back in Saxon times and that fish were raised here for her table. I've heard it said that there was another pond here sometime later, after Oliver Cromwell, in Restoration times, as well. No-one really knows, though."

"It lies very wet, alright. Look at the vegetation. There's water deeper down, I'll be bound." Mr Ralph pointed out the patches of rush and yellow flag as they pushed their way through head-high nettles growing in the few glades amongst the dense ranks of goat willow. A pheasant clattered and whirred into the air and a robin sang from one of the alders. There was a pleasant smell of wetness and growth all around the two men as they pioneered forward. On either side of the dell, the parkland rose gently, towards an extensive wood to the north and open grazing to the south.

"Look, there's a trout...and another." Mr Ralph pointed into the shallow brook. "They must be up to spawn. You told me this little stream joins a bigger one further down."

"Yes. the Don, which becomes the Nadder down beyond the mill."

Following the bank of the stream as best they could, they reached a point where the ground suddenly rose in a long bank, broken by the brook channel. A sturdy oak plank bridge, strong enough to carry a loaded cart, bridged the gap. A track stretched right and left, horse-and-cart width from the gate at the top of the field, but no more than a pasture footpath up the hill towards a just visible church tower. There was a small, apparently newly-built barn to their left, the destination of the track, with straw bales glimpsed through the half-open door.

The Saxon Ponds

"That's the footpath to the next village," puffed Horace, pointing left, slightly breathless from the effort of struggling through the undergrowth and up to the top of what could have once been a dam. "That's St Mary's you can see on the hill." He put an exploratory hand up to his cheek, where a spiteful twig had lashed it. "It's a path that's been used by local people for as long as anyone can remember. Beyond that church is the lane to Shaftesbury. I do the walk as far as the upper village quite often. It gives me great pleasure as well as being fine exercise when I feel that I need it. You can see the whole valley from the top of that pasture."

He pointed to the barn. "That belongs to my tenant, Farmer Pitman. He told me that when they came to build it, they found what looked like stone footings, as if there'd been a building there centuries ago. Saxon times, perhaps. Who can tell? But I do like to think I may be following in ancient footsteps."

Where they stood, looking upstream, with the old rectory behind them, and the barn to their left, another wilderness of reeds, willow and nettles stretched into the distance. On each side, the valley sides rose steeply, to sheep-grazed pasture on the one side and a substantial wood on the other.

"Hm. This looks like a second pond." Horace sensed the enthusiasm beneath Mr Ralph's matter-of-fact Lincolnshire tones. This was a man who thoroughly enjoyed his job. "I've seen enough for now, I think. There's no need to push our way through all that vegetation, but it looks like an ideal site. We'll leave that to the surveyors if you decide to commission us."

Over a convivial lunch, the two men agreed terms. Ford's would do the surveying and propose a detailed plan, with recommendations about the most suitable fish, plants and trees. Local people would do the job. Charges were reasonable, thought Horace as he and Mr Ralph shook hands on the deal.

Later, at family supper, Horace waxed lyrical about the day's experience to his son, daughters and grandchildren. Adelaide smiled inwardly at her husband's enthusiasm. Now, he had another pet

The Saxon Ponds

project, and she knew better than to express any doubts, such as the dangers of deep water for young children. Dutifully, she nodded agreement.

In the days that followed Horace made enquiries about local people able to cope with such an intimidating task and came up with just one name: Sampson's from the appropriately named Compton Abbas, the 'Abbess's valley enclosure', as the Saxons had described it, a village just seven miles away. Mr Sampson visited and gave every impression of competence and keenness, though he looked uncomfortable in a suit, Horace thought. He had done such work before, though on a smaller scale, and knew the pitfalls to avoid. He could be free for the work sometime in February. Horace engaged him on the spot.

At last, a letter arrived from Ford's announcing the imminent arrival of the surveyors. On a crisp, sunny day, with the first October nip of frost in the air, Horace himself drove the family carriage down to Semley railway station to collect them. True to form, he was a little late. He found them on the otherwise deserted platform, surrounded by their heavy haversacks and poles, one of the two leaning patiently on a theodolite. They were heavily bearded, ruddy-featured and cheerful, with accents even more pronounced than Mr Ralph's.

"We were startin' to get a bit worried, zur," said the chap leaning on the theodolite. "Thought you'd forgotten uz or we'd got off at the wrong place. I'm Jem Folkes and this little fella is Bob Simmonds."

Rough and ready they may have looked and sounded, but they certainly knew their job, as Horace found out the next morning, when he kept them company on that first bit of surveying. Rather hesitantly, he'd asked if he could help and soon found himself holding a red-topped pole and getting into all sorts of awkward places trying to follow their instructions.

Although he had felt clumsy and amateurish during that long and tiring day, Jem and Bob seemed to accept him as part of the

The Saxon Ponds

team and that evening all three sat close to the red-brick inglenook and warmed themselves by the welcoming open fire at 'The New Inn', where he'd booked beds and victuals for them. After a pint or two of porter, they fell to yarning about their job, the places they'd been to, country-wide it seemed, and the eccentric landowners they'd met – "Present company excepted, of course, zur!" They told him about Mr Ford's Lincolnshire farm at Caistor and the fish he raised by the thousand in his great stew ponds, about the hosts of water plants he grew – "Yellow irises, reeds and kingcups, water lilies and all sorts o' things" – and about how popular their services had become over recent years. Business was good. "We've got carps as long as your arm. Roach and rudd, tench and perch...trout too if that's your interest. And why not? They make a tasty supper or breakfast especially when you've caught 'em yoursen."

Horace felt their enthusiasm seep into him, not that he needed any boost to his keenness and impatience to get the project started. That evening, late for dinner and aware of reproachful looks all round because of it, he talked enthusiastically to Adelaide and the family, his words falling over each other he had so much to say.

"Shall we have a boat, Grandfather?" asked young Horace, daughter Adelaide's boy, jumping up and down in his seat with excitement.

"Indeed we shall, my boy, with a proper landing stage. And an island for picnics and adventures. I'll teach you all to row like champions..." though truth to tell he had little idea of how to handle an oar. At Cambridge he had avoided the boating "hearties", as he called them, and his venturing on the water had been only as a passenger reclining on a cushion with Adelaide in a punt on 'the Backs', with the white stone splendour of King's College as a backdrop.

He was taken over completely by his new enthusiasm; all doubts about affordability had vanished, and indeed his earlier hesitations had been those of a man naturally prone to doubts rather than one occasioned by the actual state of his bank balance.

The Saxon Ponds

Ten days passed. Horace waited impatiently for the plans to arrive from Ford's; Robin, the red-tunicked postman, had an expectant welcome every day. At last, his pony clip-clopping up to the servants' entrance, he came bearing an impressive envelope, smiling broadly in anticipation of Horace's pleasure. "Here it is at last, Mr Chapman!" he said.

In his study, Horace eagerly opened the large envelope. A booklet dropped to the floor with a bang. It seemed to be a catalogue, but beyond picking it up and placing it on the desk, he ignored it in his enthusiasm to examine the plans, two copies as requested of the suggested changes to his land, one for Mr Sampson, the other for himself. He saw that Mr Ralph was proposing not one lake but two, using the old, raised track as the site for the dam separating them. A fine island graced the lower pond, he saw: "revetted with weathered brick," the legend ran. He wondered about that strange word. A timber landing stage in the north-east corner of this lake fulfilled his promise to his grandchildren, with direct access from the croquet lawn and the pets' cemetery. He must set about finding a boat-builder, perhaps down in Poole he thought. He imagined a graceful skiff, in summer's day blue, moored to the landing stage post, ready for untold adventures.

What plants and fish should he have? He suddenly remembered the booklet, hidden beneath the plans on his desk. Sinking into his comfortable club chair, he opened his next prize. As he had guessed, it was indeed a catalogue, itemising all the stock and services Mr Ford offered. Horace settled down to indulge his fancies, but quickly realised that, as far as the plants were concerned, without advice he was lost in the welter of Latin names. His knowledge of fish, too, was modest. Should he stock with carp...or pike...or bream...or trout? Reluctantly he laid the catalogue aside. He needed more advice.

The work began on a dry February Monday, with just a hint of spring in the air. It was a very different Mr Sampson who greeted Horace at door, no longer suited and hatted for interview but sturdy

The Saxon Ponds

and somehow taller in heavy work-clothes and boots, much more at his ease and eager to begin.

"First we'll clear the vegetation ready for the digging," he grinned. "Then we can really get down to work. The next job'll be to dig a bypass channel for the brook so we can excavate without having to worry about too much water."

Long afterwards, in retirement in Hastings, Horace often described the making of the lakes to his friends of the chess club. It came to be his main topic of conversation as he looked back more and more nostalgically at his past. He recalled how within just a few days trees and bushes had been felled and two great bonfires had sent billows of smoke in the direction of the church on the hill. Suddenly the ground was bare. That much he could remember clearly, and Adelaide's distress at the suddenly desolate landscape.

His memory of detail had begun to leave him in those last years; some things, though, he remembered clearly, like snapshots in an album. He never tired of talking about the rough, powerful men who had dug the lakes. To him, a gentleman who seldom soiled his hands, they were like another race of beings. Sampson had told him that each and every one of his diggers could shift tons of dirt in a day. "Strongest men in Europe they are. Give 'em half an hour at midday for a drink and snap, and they'll go on till dark, take their money and drink it away at the pub, and then come up fresh as daisies for the morrow. They're hard men right enough...shouldn't like to cross 'em. Treat 'em right, though, and they'll work like Trojans for you."

Horace remembered being struck by the fact that they dug in silence but for the odd curse at a stubborn rock and the 'chunk' of the great spades. Muscles bulged, skin glistened. Just occasionally, a man would pause, straighten his back, take off his dirty neckerchief and wipe the sweat from his eyes. Otherwise, they worked in untiring unison: 'chunk', lift, turn, dump; 'chunk', lift, turn, dump; 'chunk', lift, turn, dump. Like machines, Horace thought.

The Saxon Ponds

There had been horse-drawn carts that carried the dirt up the hill and dumped unsightly heaps of mud that for months covered his fields; and the notable team of shire horses that pulled the long waggons full of massive stones, bricks, loads of cement and sand and gravel down the track to the workplace. Then there was the building of the dams and the fine brickwork of the tunnel under the track.

Horace particularly enjoyed describing how the top dam was built, how they had dug a trench along the line of the footpath, from side to side of the lake-to-be and a bit beyond, so deeply that the sides had to be shored up for safety. Mr Sampson had explained how, at some time in the past, dark green clay had been used to make what was, more and more obviously, the dam of an old pond, but that in the past it had been laid atop the greensand, with no foundation. "There would've been more water flowing in those days, so a few leaks wouldn't have mattered too much – but it's not sound practice."

Sampson's men had needed to dig deeper into the greensand and then backfill with clay to ensure a watertight footing. Horace had been intrigued by the way in which the clay was replaced in the ditch, in shallow layers, each one patiently consolidated by heavy boots and rammers. Gradually the navvies, at first deep down in the ditch, had re-appeared above the surface as the clay accumulated: heads first, then head and shoulders, then waists, then legs. That was a picture Horace never forgot.

He told his listeners about his excitement as the first boards clunked into place in the iron runners of the sluices and the way the water level inched higher and higher.

And the island! Ah, he never tired of talking about the island in the House Lake, with its ruddy-brown Gillingham brick revetting – that was the new word he liked to say and enjoyed explaining – and the way his grandchildren had picnicked on it after noisy voyages in the blue-hulled skiff he'd had built down in Poole.

The Saxon Ponds

He had fond memories of Adelaide, dressed in a summer dress of the palest primrose yellow with matching broad-brimmed hat, reclining in the skiff like the Lady of Shalott, complete with elegant parasol. He remembered teaching the grandchildren to swim, too, and how they had loved to sit on the landing stage, dangling their feet in the clear, brown-tinged water of his new lake.

To the end of his days, Harold would tell those stories to anyone who would listen, nostalgic for his elegant house and gardens deep in the Wiltshire countryside. All bitterness at the religious controversy that had driven him from that beautiful old village church had left him. He remembered only the good times: his fine house and his lakes, the white water lilies and the bright flag irises and kingcups bright against the water and the exotic rhododendrons that he himself had planted around the House Lake, feeling the complete countryman in his stiff new corduroy trousers and work boots. The memories flooded back and his audience smiled, happy to indulge the memories of their much-loved president.

"Tell us more, Harold," they'd say. "Tell us about the trout and how you learned to catch them."

"My older brother Peter taught me," he would say, sipping his vintage port and reclining at his ease after a filling meal. "He bought me a rod and reel from Hardy's - nothing but the best for Peter. He had to be patient, too, because it's tricky, you know, learning how to cast a fly and I'm a bit ham-fisted. But in the end I managed to get a line out straight enough. I had plenty of practice. Somehow fishing caught my fancy, almost as much as chess."

His listeners would smile disbelievingly; his enthusiasm for that game was legendary. "But come to the fish, Harold. Tell us about that big trout."

It was a well-worn tale. "You'll remember Ralph and I saw those little trout in the brook, when we were exploring the wet ground? Well, quite a lot of them were still there after the lakes were full and they grew fast, as Ralph said they would in a new lake. They

The Saxon Ponds

spawned every year, too, in the shallows between the two lakes, so there were plenty of fish, right up till the time I sold up."

He always looked very sad at this point and his listeners would show their sympathy. "There was one big old fella that I tried for many a time. He was always by the island, but he knew too much for me many a time. I'd see him particularly when the mayflies were up. He must have been all of three pounds, I thought. I had him one evening just on dark, on a little black gnat. Two pounds 14 ounces he weighed, so I wasn't far out. He ate well, too. I missed him once he'd gone, though a smaller one soon took his special place.

"I do miss those summer evenings. Everything quiet but for the swish of the line and the singing of the birds and the laughing of my grandchildren playing in the garden.

"What I don't think I've told you," - and his listeners smiled knowingly at each other, because he had, many times - "is how we stocked Legg Lake, the one upstream of the second dam. Ralph said why not try rainbow trout though they were great wanderers and we might lose them downstream, which in fact we did eventually. They were tasty on a plate while they lasted. We put in a fish called tench as well – I'd never heard of them; olive green they were, with a little red eye – and the grandchildren fished for them with a rod and line that Morgan the butler had. They used worms for bait – ugh, couldn't abide the thought of that myself – and sometimes brought a big one home to cook. Didn't like the taste much but the boys enjoyed them."

However, the tales that he told over and over again to anyone that would listen were far from everything that was in his heart. There was something that he had shared with no-one, a secret he knew that he could never explain. In changing the landscape of the valley, he too had been altered. His faith had been unshaken since he was old enough to think for himself but it had been an academic faith rather than one felt with his whole being. His years by the ponds had slowly but surely opened his eyes to the glories of

The Saxon Ponds

Creation, a confirmation of everything that had led him to enter the Church.

It had been as if his eyes had been opened afresh. Like his favourite poet, Gerard Manley Hopkins, that strange Jesuit poet-priest, he began to see God in everything around him. The "rose-moles all in stipples upon trout that swim" filled him with wonder as he looked more closely at them. He marvelled at the sound of the tawny owl in the ancient oak at dusk; at the glow-worms that showed him the way home after his evening hours by the water; at the soft-footed roedeer that came to drink and that he disturbed in those misty early times when sleep had deserted him; at the dawn chorus so loud in the spring; at the wildflowers whose colour and shape he had never really looked at before. All became for him manifestations of the Great Creator.

As Hopkins had done in in Inversnaid, he came to value "the wildness and the wet" of Legg Pond and the secluded valley beyond. He saw simple things with a new vision: the white underside of willow leaves blown by the wind, the spears of the early flowers of the pond sedge, yellow–tipped with pollen, the subtle colours and febrile energy of the darting, hovering dragonflies, the swooping swallows and martins in the autumn, even the silence of the ice-bound water in the depths of winter.

Like Hopkins, too, he saw how this was a glory that was of the moment, that it was not fixed, that it no doubt had changed over hundreds of years. He wondered how those who had come before him in the valley had felt about this favoured place: what creatures they had seen and heard, whether they in their primitive way had been aware that this was the abundance of a god manifested. He felt himself at the end of perhaps a long line of explorers to whom wonders had been revealed, like Cortez "silent, upon a peak in Darien."

He would settle back in the deep leather chair, eyes closed, dreaming of his Wiltshire days. His friends would leave him undisturbed.

The Saxon Ponds

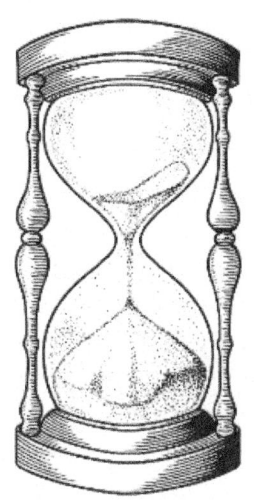

INTERLUDE

Thus Horace Chapman passed his last few years, away from his beloved Wiltshire home. He became the leading light of the Hastings and St Leonards Chess Club and eventually succumbed to pneumonia in 1907.

The Wiltshire house and land he had once owned passed into the hands of one Sir James Pender, baronet, the founder of Cable and Wireless, yachtsman and Conservative Party politician, who further improved the property. He lived in his Wiltshire home until his death in 1921 and was buried in the graveyard of the village church where Horace had once been the rector.

After this, the trail runs cold. We do not know who owned the house but it is known that during the Second World War it was used as a convalescent home for wounded soldiers. We also know that it was somehow available for Anthony Eden, a disgraced Prime Minister, to rent for a year in 1957. It and its land were acquired by Rank, Hovis MacDougall in 1968 for use as an experimental farm

The Saxon Ponds

but sold without its land to the Brewers Society as a training centre in 1969. Private buyers in 1990 inherited its 35 bedrooms and fine gardens, but not the ponds.

Here, for the moment, our interest in the house fades. During this time, the fate of the ponds remains a mystery; most likely it is a story of neglect and nature's attempt to turn them into dry land, as is the wont of things.

By the 1970s, the land, including the ponds, had passed into the hands of a family newly come from Ireland. They grazed their Connemara ponies on the valley slopes and their tenant farmer used the fields for his young cattle. The family's thoughts turned to the boggy areas that had once been ponds. Could clear water be brought back in the place of mud?

An attempt was made. At first, modern machinery made light of the dredging. But problems arose that the contractors felt unable to solve. The sluices leaked, the mud seemed bottomless; estimates soared. Half done, the ponds waited for more sympathetic attention.

Their story resumes in the early 1970s, at the January committee meeting of the local angling club, with Tommy Suttle, the town pharmacist, white-haired and red-faced, in the Chair, supported by Bob Machin, accountant, the Hon. Treasurer with funds to spare, and Pete Rolfe, schoolmaster, the Hon. Secretary, who knew how to restore ponds. The latter had an exciting opportunity to put before the members.

The Saxon Ponds

CHAPTER THREE

March 1975 - 1992

Pete Rolfe had the floor under Any Other Business. "I've had an interesting 'phone call, gentlemen. From a Miss Miller. She has two ponds just inside the Wiltshire border that need some TLC. Originally, they belonged to the old rectory but now her family has them. She's offering a seven-year, rent-free lease if we can restore them."

"Yes, she's been in touch with me, too," beamed Tommy. "Sounds promising. I suggest the Pete and Bob do a recce for us and report back at the next meeting."

There was no disagreement. A year or two earlier there might have been more hesitation, but with the recent experience of creating a fine two-lake fishery in a brickyard close to their hometown, confidence was high.

***

The Saxon Ponds

Bob and Pete looked an ill-assorted pair, the short and long of it, as they made their Barboured way down the track to the ponds, but they were a good team, Bob with his accountancy skills and his ability to find a way to finance grand schemes, and Pete well-experienced in saving neglected pieces of water.

On their way through the village, a hamlet really, they had passed an ancient church and fine houses built of local stone. The air seemed full of promise. They felt on the brink of a momentous discovery.

Beyond a five-barred gate, the track to the ponds lay through rich pasture. To their right, the top of the valley was clothed with extensive woodland – Berrywood Copse, Blanche had called it. To their left, atop the meadow, three neglected cottages crowned the skyline.

The great balks of timber that formed the track in the approach to the dam between the two ponds reminded Pete of the strange wooden road he had walked along in a remote part of Ireland many years before. The massive timbers continued over the dam, from where the two men could see one of the two ponds. The other, behind them, was hidden by trees and bushes.

There was water in the one pond they could see, though it was obviously shallow. Two islands - hardly islands, more like heaps of soil abandoned during the aborted attempt at dredging – dominated the view. Willow and alder crowded the banks and a great bed of reeds clogged the far end of the pond, where presumably the feeder stream entered and dropped its silt. Two or three dilapidated boards remained in the sluice runners, holding back what water there was.

But Pete, at least, was not discouraged by what he saw. The flow of water over the boards was strong, even after the dry spell that had lasted through most of the early winter. Peering over the brickwork of the dam, gazing into the clear brown water, he saw what he had hoped – snails feeding on the green algae growing on the stone of the sluice, a few shrimps and plenty of what looked like

The Saxon Ponds

small mayfly nymphs on the sandy silt of the pond bed. Water quality must be good.

A buzzard called loud and clear as if in welcome. The two men watched for a moment as the big bird quartered the field leading up to the wood, broad wings catching every updraught, tip feathers stiff like so many fingers. It seemed a good omen.

"It looks difficult to walk round that pond," said Bob. "Quite a lot of work to do there."

"Let's find the lower pond then, Bob," suggested Pete. "Perhaps we can make our way through that old cattle stall."

Opposite a barn half-filled with straw and with a dozen young steers inquisitively poking their heads over a barrier, were seven abandoned stalls, in red brick, with rotting roofs and stout metal-barred doors welded tight by rust and disuse, and crammed with elder, brambles and nettles. One, though, was promising, less overgrown than the others. The door responded at last to the two men's strength, and they were through into the stall. Four metal rings in the wall made it like a dungeon where unspeakable deeds were done, but the wooden back wall had long rotted away and Bob and Pete scrambled into the area beyond. A holly bush, still loaded with berries, and two giant laurel bushes temporarily barred their way. Beyond, suddenly in full view, was the second pond.

Like the first they had seen, this one had two islands projecting from shallow water. One of them was more than just a heap of spoil, though, to judge from the rhodendron and tall alders growing from it. Perhaps it had been part of the original design.

In other ways, too, this pond was different from the upper one, which had been a feature in a wilderness. The holly and laurel bushes suggested that what they saw now had once been part of a garden. The opposite bank was dominated by several tall Scots pines and a clump of three big alders but on the bank the two men were on a series of huge rhododendrons suggested a plan and long-ago cultivation, an impression supported by the glimpse of the light-coloured façade of a big house through the trees.

The Saxon Ponds

With difficulty, Bob and Pete made their way through nettles and brambles to the sluice, constructed of great blocks of local stone, and, as in the other pond, with just three boards holding back 18" of water. Beyond were lawns and a neatly maintained pets' cemetery with four headstones.

On their way back to the farmyard, they were aware of the smell of slurry. Following their noses, they found a shallow ditch into which the barn clearly drained and which would need attention if pollution was not to be a problem. It was not a serious issue, as what they saw next indicated. Bob had gone to look more closely at the shallow stream leading from the upper pond and feeding into this one.

"There are fish here," he said excitedly. Pete joined him on the bank. Perhaps half a dozen brown trout, each one half a pond or so in weight, were questing the current. "They must have swum up from the Nadder to spawn."

The sight of these healthy fish removed any doubts that the Hon. Treasurer and Hon. Secretary might have had. Their report would be positive.

***

There were plenty of volunteers, a dozen for that first Sunday morning's work party, after the previous day's AGM. It was early April and the promise of spring was in the air. The lower pond was loud with banter and laughter and the crackling of bonfires. The smell of wood smoke filled the air. The green and oily cuttings from the once-towering rhododendrons burned well. The two roaring fires, on opposite banks, with their fierce heat, made short work of both the rhododendron cuttings and the branches from the pollarded willows and alders. The dead wood that had littered the banks after years of neglect had added fuel to the fires. After just three hours even Ron, the lugubrious Match Secretary, a man difficult to please, looked happy at what he saw.

Two more such sessions saw light and life return to the pond. The tall Scots pines had been sold and felled by contractors, overhanging

The Saxon Ponds

trees and bushes cut back hard and the gloomy, oppressive rhododendrons down to five feet or so. The three boards in the sluice had been removed and only a small stream, cutting ever deeper into the silt, remained for the trout to enjoy. The silt of ages was exposed to the light.

Ten days after that third work party, Rolfe walked the ponds with the family Labrador, as he did at least twice a week. This time, though, was different. The excavator had arrived. The huge, yellow-cabbed machine was there in the yard, out of proportion with its surroundings, like a Diplodocus in a dining room. With a mixture of trepidation and excitement, Pete sensed great power ready to be unleashed.

On the first day of the new week, he was there punctually at 8am to chat with Alan, the driver, a man that he came to like and know well over the following years. Now, though, he was an unknown quantity: tall, slim and cheerful, with a rich Wiltshire burr to his voice. A man to have confidence in, Pete felt, not least because it was clear that he loved his job, particularly when it came to creating a pond.

The machine burst into life with a roar from the engine and a belch of exhaust smoke. "We're off, then," grinned Alan. The excavator scrunched on its caterpillar tracks away from the yard towards the distant sluice, then made a sharp left turn and entered the pond, Alan testing the way with the bucket at the end of its long boom. "Feels fine," Alan shouted from his cab. "There's solid bottom underneath this silt right enough."

Thus it proved over the next few days, except for one area where a spring entered the pond. There the mud seemed unfathomable, an area to avoid. Elsewhere the wet silt was scraped from the firm gravel and greensand that made up the bed of the pond. That which could not be landscaped into the banks and immediate surrounds was buried by a second machine in pits dug in the gently rising pasture to the north of the pond; notices were posted of the surrounding fence, threatening a muddy drowning for trespassers.

The Saxon Ponds

The silt island had been removed but the other, cleaned of its coat of mud, remained, its overhanging rhododendrons and the tall alder saplings cut back. It was protected against the erosive power of wind-lapped water by a wall of dark red Gillingham brick, unmortared but meticulously laid course on course. The crevices would be a haven for innumerable water creatures, Pete thought, all food for the fish he already imagined swimming in this new pond.

The island must once have been a grand place for children to picnic on, Pete reflected. He pictured a landing stage, summer revelry and an elegant woman reclined on the back thwart of a skiff rowed by a straw-boatered gentleman.

Brian, the club's joinery expert, had already provided elm boards cut to size for the sluice. There they were, in a neat stack, covered by a tarpaulin so that they could not dry out and warp, and with due ceremony – once the excavator had departed for the yard, awaiting the low-loader that would come to take it away – each board was carefully, with a barely concealed excitement on the part of all, slotted into the iron runners, to descend with a satisfying thud on top of the one beneath it. Immediately, it seemed, the water level began to rise, half inch by half inch.

By the end of the year, the upper pond too had been drained and dried out by the long summer days. In its turn it had been dredged and refilled. Two new ponds, each of a good half acre, awaited stocking. It would not be long before they could be fished.

Until now, things had gone well. They were about to change. Unsurprisingly perhaps, the dams had deteriorated over the 70 or 80 years since they were built. Pointing in brickwork and between the stone blocks that made up the sluices had all but disappeared, allowing water through. On the lower pond, where the dam was shorter and made up just of massive blocks of greenstone, some remedial work seemed possible and Pete spent hours filling cracks with cement mixed with a rapid-set compound. He became familiar with lugging cement and Sealocrete from the car along the bank of the pond to the sluice, climbing down below the boards and mixing

The Saxon Ponds

cement on a plastic bucket lid. He felt it warm in the hand as he forced it into the cracks before it set hard.

It worked well but there were frustrations, too. He would leave for home, well pleased that all was sealed and sound. The next day, though, when the water had topped the next board, more jets of water told him of yet more work to do. But he enjoyed those solitary sessions, sheltered from any wind by the great blocks of sandstone, hearing the trickling of water diminish minute by minute as he methodically plugged the gaps, with the moorhens and ducks for company.

A second, more serious problem was that the impact of water overflowing sluice boards had over time eroded deep holes behind the concrete sills, particularly in the upper pond, as Pete discovered when he ventured up the tunnel beneath the track. As he explored, back bent, step by step, he marvelled at the craftsmanship of the arched brickwork. Surrounded by the echo of falling water and its riverine smell, he was suddenly conscious of the weight of water held back by the boards and imagined what would have happened to him had they given way. The hole that he found was perhaps a metre deep. Did it go down below the clay of the dam? Would that lead to a leak? Filling the sump with stones might slow down the erosion. It seemed worth a try. That was an error of judgement, the result of which would become obvious in seven years' time.

Then, at the end of that first seven-year lease, with a new one agreed, the club was ready to spend more money on the ponds. It was the turn of the upper one, for some desilting at the top end and the far-too-small silt trap. Landscaping, too, and work on the dam and sluice.

There had been mutterings from members that the pond needed stocking with more fish; sport had been slow. Pete was sceptical, knowing how rich in food the pond was, which he knew must make the fish more difficult to catch. He had found plenty of snails and shrimps whenever he had raked curly-leafed pondweed from his swim or looked closely at the red willow roots in the shallow water.

The Saxon Ponds

In early spring blooms of Daphnia and Cyclops clouded the water. A much better plan than putting in more fish, he thought, was allowing those already there to grow and breed.

So he was pleased to be proved right when the net was drawn in full of a healthy crop of fine, healthy roach, carp, tench and crucians, over a 1000 of them, many good ones amongst them. These were carried down to the lower pond in buckets. As the water level dropped to a very few inches and then to next to nothing, the more intrepid members waded into the mud to rescue the few fish that remined, mostly tench that seemed no worse for the experience. Then there was time for coffee and a chat, excited discussion of the quality of the fish they had seen.

With the pond now dry, work could commence. Alan's machine attended to the desilting, while a local builder's men repointed the dilapidated sections of the dam wall, working from improvised scaffolding. New iron runners replaced the Victorian originals, now badly rusted and eroded, and brand-new elm boards were put into place, one by one, liberally proofed with water pump grease, which Pete had read would make the boards more watertight.

The water rose to the top of the fourth board and then disaster struck. The level suddenly began to drop as the water found a weak place beneath the sill and took a gurgling and giggling short-cut to the lower pond. Hearts sank with the water; there was no way the club could afford professional help for what was obviously a serious problem.

'Cometh the hour, cometh the man' though. After much scratching of heads and practical advice from a multi-talented committee, a plan of action was agreed. If the sill, the area in front of it and first few yards of the tunnel were to be concreted, the agreed plan, then a way must be found to keep water from flowing into the drained pond. Supposing they dammed the feeder brook and let the water flood the valley upstream for enough time to do the job? It entered the pond from the silt trap through a narrow channel some five feet deep, and the levels looked right.

The Saxon Ponds

The day started early, a little after first light. Working quickly, six stalwarts ranging in age from keen young men in their twenties to one near-pensioner, blocked the feeder brook with stout timber and plastic. No-one knew whether the structure would withstand the water pressure or how long they would have before the water topped the 'dam'. Quickly, the land upstream began to flood.

The sump was cleared of stones and all was ready for the pre-mix concrete lorry, which arrived promptly at noon, its driver anxious to see the last of the waterproofed, quick-setting concrete that he feared could clog his machine.

"Let's do this fast, lads," he instructed, "or it'll cost me a new lorry!"

All was noise and bustle, but everyone knew their task. From the revolving body of the lorry, the concrete ran down the chute straight into the mouth of the sluice, there to be spread with shovels and rakes, until the sump was filled, the floor of the tunnel, the sill and an area in front of it carefully levelled, a noisy vibro-poker in use all the time to expel the very last bubbles of air from the concrete, which within an hour was beginning to set hard.

With a roar of its engine and a cheerful toot on the horn, the pre-mix lorry left for the depot, its relieved driver waving goodbye, watched by six tired, mud-and-concrete-splattered volunteers. There were handshakes and backslaps all round, everyone happy and relieved that they had done a good job. Three boards were replaced, and the workers climbed wearily onto the bank of the pond. As if on cue, water overlapped the temporary dam and began to flood into the pond.

On the Sunday, seven boards were in place and the temporary dam was gradually reduced in height so that the shallow lake above it could begin to dry out. The pond rapidly filled as a result. All looked very fine.

When Rolfe walked down the track two days later, expecting to enjoy the sight of a full pond, his heart sank. He could hardly believe what he saw. Even from a hundred yards away he knew that the

The Saxon Ponds

level had dropped. Sure enough, a gurgling vortex in front of the boards showed where the water was vanishing beneath the sill. The repair work had not gone deep enough and even filling the sump with concrete had not been sufficient. All that hard work had been for nothing.

His report to the committee was gloomy, though he had a possible solution to suggest, and a week later the same gang of volunteers began a second operation, this time involving a stout polythene rick sheet and lots more hard work. Once again the water was held back, while 9" of good grey-green clay from the side of the pond formed an impermeable layer in the leak area, replacing dug-out greensand. Then followed the plastic sheet, generously overlapping the suspect area, and then another layer of puddled clay up to the level of the sill.

"That should do the trick," was the general verdict, and so it proved, though for some time Rolfe half-expected disaster when he walked the track to the ponds.

***

Angling clubs are fine institutions; there is strength in numbers, providing finance for just such opportunities as the Saxon Ponds and manpower for swim clearance and general maintenance. Many pairs of eyes mean that pollution and poaching are soon discovered.
When it comes to stocking with fish, though, having many voices and opinions can be a problem. Given the blank sheet of a new, unstocked water, everyone wants to fill it with his favourite fish: Dennis wants roach, the fish he enjoys catching on the river; Ron favours bream for his match fishermen; Bob loves fishing for tench, Bruce for carp, Tommy for rudd, Pete for crucians and perch. Some stillwater chub fishing would be novel. Why not a pike or two? Rainbow trout even.

And so the discussion had been lively at committee meetings, from the very inception of this new fishery. In the end, they listened

The Saxon Ponds

to Pete Rolfe's advice. He had been heavily involved in the creation of their fine two-lake fishery close to town and had chaired the group given the responsibility of managing it. His experience of restoring and stocking field ponds in the Vale had taught him much about balancing fish stocks and knowing which fish best went with which. He persuaded the committee that bream, the matchmen's favourite, would be a mistake in such small ponds, especially in the early days, and that perch should wait till later.

There was general agreement that tench should be one of the main fish. Crucians and common carp, each species in a separate pond, with some decent roach if they could be found, would make up the rest of the initial stock.

The club had a stock pond deep in the heart of the countryside, containing many small tench and Bob and Pete volunteered to be the first to transfer fish into the new fishery.

It is always exciting to be pioneers, and that is how they felt that June Saturday morning. They had arranged to meet at crack of dawn and the birds were singing as Pete made his way through the gap in the hedge that marked the entrance to the pond. Until very recently this had been the only stillwater fishing on the club's books and Pete was keen to try it for the first time. It had been difficult to find and it was only the clump of willows visible above the hedge and the quoik of a moorhen that led him to it.

The pond was a good one as field ponds in the Vale went, rectangular, about 40 yards long and 10 wide, with three or four feet of water as he found when he made his first cast. The water had the greenness typical of a small rich pool, with no soft weed visible. Probably the tench kept it down with their constant probing of the silt for bloodworms, Pete thought. To his left a freckle of leaves just beginning to break surface showed that floating leaved pondweed would be a problem later in the summer, one he was familiar with from his work on other ponds in the Vale.

The Saxon Ponds

"Top of the morning to you, Pete," came Bob's voice from behind him; he'd been too focussed on the pond to be aware that he had company.

Bob was a matchman by instinct; Pete was not. So the competition that followed could only ever have one winner.

"Rudd don't count, of course," grinned Bob as Pete lifted a fingerling from the surface. "Only tench!"

A couple of hours later, they lifted their respective keepnets, transferred the squirming tench to black plastic bags quarter-filled with water, and made their way to the new ponds. Slipping the tench into the lower pond seemed like the beginning of a new era. Bob and Pete watched the last of them swim away into the clear brown depth of the pond and smiled at each other.

***

The years that followed saw the fishery mature into a fine one. Fishing was limited in those early days, with just half a dozen anglers allowed on any one day. Youngsters had to be accompanied by an adult, a wise precaution, as later events proved.

The Hon. Sec. kept a diary of the times he fished the ponds and years later found pleasure in reading about those pioneering days: how the tench grew fast, to something approaching two pounds in just two summers; how, after an early setback, when a stocking of 18 young carp mysteriously died, the common carp became established and numerous; how the roach grew to nearly two pounds and the crucian carp to half that weight; how the wildlife attracted to the ponds was a constant delight. He remembered the challenge of catching even a few fish from such rich, fish-food-crammed ponds, float fishing into darkness with an illuminated float for shy-biting crucian carp and tench, bats flickering overhead and owls hooting; seeing a fox carrying a rabbit along the far bank one misty summer early morning and watching mewing buzzards over Berrywood Copse.

The Saxon Ponds

There were problems, too: weed grew to become a nuisance, Canadian pondweed in particular, and had to be raked onto the bank, often crawling with snails, invertebrates and baby fish; tench spawned prolifically and their numbers had to be controlled by seine netting; the lower pond dam continued to leak and Pete would often worry about water levels during hot, dry times.

When the time came for him to resign the secretaryship because of pressure from the day job, when education in the hilltop town was re-organised and he had new responsibilities, he found less and less time for fishing. Eventually, he lost close touch with the club and the ponds. For him, an era had come to an end.

The Saxon Ponds

The Saxon Ponds

INTERLUDE

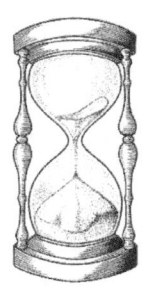

Nine years passed. Different ideas prevailed and the fishing on the ponds changed. Common carp began to dominate the water, perch were introduced, restrictions were lifted. In the Saxon hilltop town, news of what was happening just occasionally arrived. There was a rumour that it was planned to stock the ponds with bream, which idea brought a wry smile to Rolfe's face. "Each to his own," he thought, "but that won't work."

The club spent a lot of money on replacing the lower pond dam and sluice and for a time leaks became a thing of the past. All seemed well. Then came disaster.

The story varies with the teller, but the gist of it was that a couple of lads, sheltering from the rain in the bale-filled barn, dropped a cigarette end that ignited the straw and a conflagration followed. The fire brigade, called late, could do little but stand and watch, so total and well-advanced was the fire.

No one was hurt and there had been no animals there at that time, but there were consequences, nevertheless. When the club secretary visited the owner to discuss a new lease, his manner was felt to be overly forceful, as he pointed out how much the club had quite recently spent on the lower pond sluice. The upshot of that, and the accident, was that the lease was not renewed.

The Saxon Ponds

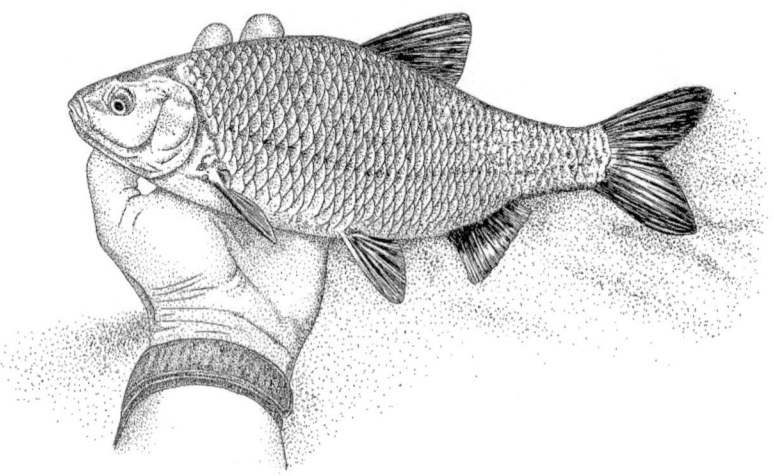

The Saxon Ponds

CHAPTER FOUR

Extracts from a Notebook and Random Thoughts

1992 to 2010

February 1992: This morning I had a phone call from B. M., totally out of the blue. "Peter Rolfe, I'm not renewing the club's lease on the ponds," she said. "Would you like to take them over?" Caught on the hop, still in pyjamas, hardly believing what I was hearing, I answered "Yes," without a single thought about the drawbacks. What an opportunity!

Awareness of a possible problem came later, over coffee, when I realised that this would be a disaster for my relations with the club. I did not want to fall out with anyone over this but there would understandably be hard feelings. I consoled myself with the thought

The Saxon Ponds

that the initiative had not come from me and therefore I had no reason to feel guilty.

May and June 1992: Yesterday the club lowered the level of the lower pond by a couple of boards and netted out the fish. Last week they did the same for the upper pond. Dates and method had been agreed over a couple of rather frosty 'phone calls. Tactfully, I did not attend either of the nettings, though I would dearly have liked to have been there. Thus, I have no idea what fish have come out.

When I visited the ponds yesterday, after the captains and the kings had left, I saw that the concrete plinth on the upper pond dam had been stripped of its wooden seat, dedicated to one of the club's oldest serving members, now deceased, who had come to love the ponds almost as much as I. I understood the club's resentment and indeed sympathised with it, but I couldn't help feeling that Dennis's ghost would have enjoyed sitting there, whoever oversaw the ponds. Now, he'd have to stand, as would I.

March 1993: I have the instincts of a fish farmer to go with those of an angler, though a fair weather, part-time one: I like to choose my day for working, something I can do now with the Saxon Ponds, as I'm going to call them. I enjoy providing the right conditions for fish to spawn and for fry to thrive and grow quickly. I enjoy too the netting and cropping, the preparation for sale and the income from it, although I am happy for most of this to go to the owner – the privilege and challenge of managing these two lovely ponds is enough. What fun!

Things have come a long way since the 1970s, when I began my quest for local stillwater fishing and restored half a dozen field ponds in the Vale, learning my skills by trial and error. I am ready for this.

My current plan for the Saxon Ponds is to raise fish for sale rather than for sport, though of course I hope to enjoy an occasional day there with rod and line, if only to check how the fish are progressing. I wonder if whoever looked after the ponds for that legendary Prioress ever did the same. And what about the Victorian creators

The Saxon Ponds

of the present ponds? Did he or she ever fish them...and for what? I suppose that I, now, will be part of the ponds' history.

Now, both ponds have been drained, dredged and refilled. I want to start with a blank canvas. The club had left some fish behind, and before I started my work, I offered them back free of charge if they came to do the netting. There was no response.

The fish that we rescued before the dredging were 100 or so common carp averaging perhaps 2lbs, biggest 7lbs, a sprinkling of young tench to 8", and a couple of thousand carp, roach, perch and bream fry, the latter confirming the rumours I had heard about the club's stocking policy.

23rd April 1993 (St George's Day and Shakespeare's birthday): It is a wonderful opportunity to have the management of two such beautiful ponds and not to have to meet anyone else's expectations, apart from the modest income promised to Blanche from the sale of fish. I am compiling a stocking list and have decided on a dozen 8" - 12" golden tench and 20 good-sized golden rudd for the upper pond; 18 green tench to 3lbs and 10 6" - 8" mirror carp for the lower one. The tench will be a mix of males and females, two to one – fortunately, tench are easy to sex. These are the brood fish from which future generations will spring. They will come from our stew ponds at 'the Wetland', so I will know they are fine healthy fish. I have chosen the species with an eye on future croppings and sales, though the carp are a self-indulgence. I wonder how big they'll grow.

Now I must wait on events.

***

The summer of '93: The ponds have been a delight. I regularly scythe a path around them, keeping on top of the nettles and enjoying the smell of cut grass and the swishing of the Turk-scythe blade. Wildflowers are plentiful – sedge and flag, bluebells, snowdrops, wood anemones, opposite leaved saxifrage, yellow loosetrife, comfrey, snowdrops, herb robert, dove-footed cranesbill, comfrey and many whose names I do not yet know. So far, there has been no real problem with algae, just some occasional scum and

The Saxon Ponds

some blanket weed. Aquatic 'weed' has steadily increased: starwort and a grass-leafed *Potamogeton* in the upper pond and starwort, some hornwort and – slightly worryingly – some growing clumps of Canadian pondweed in the lower. These plants have appeared naturally – I've not introduced any, so where do they come from? Both ponds have, after all, been drained and dredged.

I find it fascinating, the way in which life so quickly comes to a new pond – one of the main reasons that I do the job, I suppose. I introduced modest numbers of water snails of several kinds and already the gelatinous eggs are on the underside of the young white water lily leaves. When I shine a powerful torch into the water at dusk there are thousands of insects and bugs crowding the shallows. I have seen this phenomenon many times, but it still amazes me. Toad tadpoles are there in their millions by May. Dragonflies and damselflies shucks decorate the spikes of pond sedge. Swallows and martins hunt the midges that drift in ever-shifting clouds above the water. Huge, slightly pink masses of *Daphnia* crowd both ponds, plentiful food for the mostly invisible fish. Huge clouds of midges tell me that there will be plenty of bloodworms for fish to eat.

So far, I have glimpsed only the golden rudd, their fry, too, in both ponds, though this fish was stocked only in the upper one. There are plenty of duck, mallard and tufties. Canadian geese have nested on the island and the male guards their territory against the numerous moorhens and quarrelsome coots. Of course, there are herons. Once I saw three at the top pond inflow, a family group no doubt, after frogs or baby fish? I seldom visit the ponds without seeing the bright flash of a kingfisher.

March 1994: Stocked the upper pond with 18 crucian carp and added half a dozen roach to the lower pond. I do wonder about the consequences of those actions, whether there will be hybridisation, for example. But I think that the timing is right.

I've tethered four straw bales in each pond, hoping to nip any algal bloom in the bud. Other people's experience of this is mixed

The Saxon Ponds

and the advice contradictory. Should I put in the bales as they are? – which is what I've decided to do – or split the bales and use the straw loose in a confined bay? – the work involved in this has put me off this idea. Fingers crossed, then!

The summer of 1994: Yesterday, I fished the ponds for the first time after my 'takeover'. It is always an exciting experience, that cast into a 'new' water, finding out how the various species have fared. How big are the fish now? Are they in good condition? Every dip of the red-topped float was like the opening of a door to a treasure chamber – what fish would come next to the net?

It was one of those still August mornings, with just enough hazy sunshine to promise that the settled spell of weather was not yet over. I made myself comfortable by the three alders, looking south across the lower pond towards the field patrolled by a solitary llama – I kid you not. There were other surprises, too, that first morning's fishing.

First, the carp. I put them in two growing seasons ago – counting this summer – at 8" maximum. Now they are well over three pounds in weight, glowing with health and fighting hard on the light tackle I use. That is an impressive growth rate for such young fish. Then I caught a gold tench of similar size and a golden rudd that was obviously one of the original stockees. The surprise is that these fish were put into the upper pond and I was fishing the lower! I knew that fry would move downstream, perhaps originally as fertilised eggs, or swept over the top pond boards after heavy rain, indeed I'd already seen rudd fry in both ponds. These, though, were big fish, well able to resist the current.

Then, there were the crayfish. Slow, difficult-to-hit bites had alerted me, though at first I half-wondered whether they were from very small crucian carp – as I then called them, not knowing any better than to follow convention and call them 'carp', which of course they are not, except in the widest sense of being *Cyprinidae* like roach and bream.

The Saxon Ponds

When I began to catch crayfish regularly, lifting the nasty, black, rattly things from the water, I knew that there was another problem in the making. Not only would they compete with the fish for food; they dig holes in the bank and I can do without more leaks.

Fast forward to 1996: I've worked out a routine for cropping the ponds: it is too difficult to sell fish retail: holding the fish ready for the buyer is a problem, requiring tanks and aeration, so I sell them to a dealer and let him do the netting. Prices are lower, of course, but the logistics much simpler.

I am always conscious of history and my insignificant place in it. I wonder how all this would have been done in the past, before machinery was available. Who had made the ponds in the first place? How would they have been dug? In both Anglo-Saxon and Victorian times, and perhaps those events inbetween, lost in the mists of time, there would have been plenty of cheap labour, men with strong backs, I suppose, using wheelbarrows and shovels.

And for cropping the fish in King Alfred's time? – a primitive net, made from some sort of plant fibre, perhaps, for the catching; and then, for transport, willow baskets, filled with wet reeds and rushes, and ox-drawn carts to carry everything. What fish? Everyone thinks of carp first, but before that it must have been tench and bream. Eels would have been abundant, too. They would have been tasty but I'm not sure about slimy old bream, even tench, though they are eaten in Europe to this day. I have often seen them displayed for sale in an Italian market beside Lago di Garda and Lago di Orta. I bet that the Victorian builder of the ponds would have stocked them with trout, the gentleman's fish.

I enjoy speculating like this because in my own small way, I'm continuing that tradition. Dennis, the man who buys the fish, certainly is a throwback to the past in his command of rich Anglo-Saxon expletives.

Perhaps I'll put the ponds' story in a book one day.

The Saxon Ponds

Christmas 1997 – the Year of the Crayfish: This year I resolved to deal with the crayfish plague. Trapping began in April, with a proper little mesh trap Chris, the gardener at the big house, found in his employer's shed. According to Chris, the brook below the bottom pond was "Full of the pesky things," which I can well believe – they must make their way up from the young river into which the brook flows a couple of hundred yards away. Perhaps that means that however many we trap we'll never get on top of the problem!

Things started slowly enough in the spring: occasionally, one would be tempted by the luncheon meat, which I tried first. As the water warmed the darn creatures became more active: the record was 35 at one go and 600 in total before the draining and cropping made further trapping unnecessary.

I experimented with bait - luncheon meat, smoked haddock, a sacrificed rudd – but in the end relied on their cannibalism, one or two crayfish corpses each time. I sold a few of the creatures to a local restaurant, hoping for a bonanza, but trade was disappointing, so slaughter it had to be, except when friends occasionally begged a few.

Once or twice small fish, tench or rudd, were in the trap, though it was unlikely they were there after the bait. A fine eel of a pound and a half, on the other hand, could have been. It is a rare fish here nowadays and, sadly, I have never seen any other sign of them, even when the ponds have been drained.

We did just that in October, when we had to empty the pond for work to be done on the sill. Richard – struggling to free himself from the thigh-deep mud – saw dozens of crayfish between the gaps in the island brickwork, poking out their black heads and no doubt wondering where the water had gone.

Looking back 1998 – 2010: We have never again suffered a plague like that of 1997. Just occasionally, one of those very slow bites, with the float holding just beneath the surface, makes me think of those bad old days, but now it is much more likely to be from a

The Saxon Ponds

super-subtle crucian than a rattly crayfish. Looking back on the trapping, it was part of the job that I did not enjoy. Of course, red-clawed Signal crayfish are intruders and the Environment Agency tell us that they must be culled but squashing dozens of them at a time is not my idea of fun.

I wonder if in the far distant past the native crayfish thrived in the same way. I like to imagine when the wildlife of the ponds was new and unspoiled. What birds and beasts the Anglo-Saxons must have seen, everywhere, all around them! It would have been like that for the Mountain Men in the books I read about 1820s America, pioneers in a land of natural wonders. Even in our man-spoiled times, I had the same feeling as a boy in post-war Essex; fishing in Ireland in the 60s, as well – listening to the corncrakes, the bitterns and the snipe, and fishing for wild fish in wild waters.

I suppose that the work I have done with tiny field ponds, bigger lakes, too, has been my way of trying to turn back the clock to unspoiled times.

Two memories in particular stand out for those years. There was the drowned roedeer that I found in the upper pond. I cast a pike line and dragged it to the bank. It had no mark upon it. Could such a sure-footed creature slip into a pond?

Then there was the wing-injured cormorant that I eventually shot with my powerful airgun. I briefly felt pity for the creature as it swam by, evading my clumsy aim. Then it dived and emerged with one of my prized crucians in its beak; that sealed its fate. Eventually, perhaps waterlogged and exhausted, it let me get close enough to administer the *coup de grace.*

I once took an injured heron to the Shaftesbury vet for treatment. A cormorant, though, was a different kettle of fish, if you'll pardon the expression!

A Monster Carp Interlude: Looking back on it now, it is hard to believe that the Saxon Ponds were once a very good carp water. My 'dabblers' would be surprised that Pete could allow carp there, I

The Saxon Ponds

think; one reason for their fishing the ponds is that there are NO carp, apart from Moby Dick, that is, whose story I shall reveal later. There had been some carp in the ponds since the days of the angling club, and I also introduced a small number of the then-fashionable Dinklesbuehl variety, in the rather vague hope of producing an interesting strain of mirror carp if they cross-bred with the original stock.

Carp are a popular species with anglers and young fish then had a ready sale. My carp management had always been haphazard, though – they were there as just one of several species. In 1998 that was about to change.

We had drained and dredged the lower pond in the early winter of 1997, as I have described, and I left it fallow to build up invertebrate numbers from the brook until the end of March 1998. I knew that the carp in the upper pond had spawned well and the idea came to me that I would devote the lower pond to growing them on, excluding them from the top one to allow the other species to grow faster.

In the netting on 22nd March the next year, we moved 1200 3" mostly mirror carp to the lower pond, together with 12 adult fish between five and ten pounds. I planned to feed the fish there throughout the summer and crop out for sale in the winter of 1998. About 1000 3"-4" golden rudd went with them, as well as half a dozen perch of about one pound in weight. I never stocked with rudd again, preferring roach.

I found it interesting that, despite carp and crucians having lived fin-in-fin together for a few years, there were very few hybrids found when we netted. I'm beginning to think that the danger of crossbreeding these two species is exaggerated, though I've found reference to this hybrid in books as far back as Victorian times – the f1 is not just a modern phenomenon. Certainly, in my experience, the main drawback of having carp and crucians in the same small water is inter-species competition. Carp are greedy fish and crucians

The Saxon Ponds

super-efficient at breeding, so they're perhaps not good for each other in small waters like the Saxon Ponds.

The upper pond now contained tench, roach and crucians, plus two small grass carp, inherited from Brookwater Aquatics. Tench ran to well over three pounds, while the crucians – as I have now come to call them – were just 5"-7", pristine young fish. Just 20 good roach weighing up to a pound added variety and no doubt would spawn later in the year.

I fed the carp in the lower pond with soaked organic wheat about every third day, a routine but not a chore. I enjoyed the smell and texture of the grain as I threw it into each of the three feeding stations with my child's yellow sandcastle spade. It was exciting to see the big fish come swirling to my very feet once they had learned that I was the bringer of good things. I loaded two black plastic bins with my store of wheat and always had one bucketful soaking in readiness for the next feed. I found that leaving the corn to soak too long made the whole experience rather pongy!

That summer I fed 18 half-hundredweight bags of corn to the carp and by the early winter the numerous small fish were a fine and healthy 8". I sold them, together with the rudd, at the end of that growing season.

Already, though, I was tired of managing a monoculture and my plans were set to change yet again: angling was going to take over from fish farming, but with a difference.

The world of angling was developing along lines that I found regrettable. Commercial fisheries and syndicate waters were all the rage and at the former, facilities were constantly improving, if that is the word: ponds and lakes had platforms, toilets, cafes and tackle shops. Everywhere, it seemed, carp was king: bivvies, banks of matching rods and bait alarms were the norm. It sometimes seemed as if angling had become mechanised. 'Bagging up' and the pursuit of the biggest, almost always carp, were the new norm. Many anglers had known nothing but carp fishing

The Saxon Ponds

This was all foreign to me and I knew that there must be plenty of other, older anglers that felt the same, who were happy catching a wider range of species in more natural surroundings, traditional fishing if you like. I knew that the Saxon Ponds could provide just that, with just a few big carp to be the elusive monsters we used to dream about in the old days.

The dozen big carp that remained in the lower pond had company in the following year, when both ponds were netted again. There were now 14 of them – the two extra were ones that we had missed until then in the upper pond – together with 60 tench and 75 crucians. In the upper pond, there were 150 crucians, 80 nice roach, 50 tench to two and a half pounds, plus the two grass carp, a pound or two heavier than when we last weighed them. Not that I communicated those cold statistics to my slowly growing group of anglers; it would have seemed too mathematical and, anyway, half the fun of angling lies in the fact that you don't know what is under the surface and I would not want to spoil speculation.

Just one or two of my hand-picked, interviewed and then approved anglers went after the big carp in the lower pond. Ian, the keenest, spent many an hour there, trying to catch all of them in turn, keeping a record of the scale patterns of individual fish. In the end the biggest was well over 20 pounds, a huge fish for such a small pond, with back-up doubles for company. All these fish had grown to that size in two half-acre ponds over more than a decade; they were not introduced fish, except as 8" youngsters.

Michael, my friend of many, many years, occasionally visited us from New Zealand, and could never resist fishing for those difficult carp. Their movements during the day were predictable but getting them to take a bait was more challenging. In the early hours, they cruised the dam area in the lower pond, enjoying the sun. Late afternoon and evening saw them at the other end of the pond, where the water was quite shallow, no more than a couple of feet. There was a bed of reedmace, just a few square yards in area, and the carp seemed to enjoy being close to it. The reedmace would often

The Saxon Ponds

quiver and shake from the attentions of feeding fish and great ripples would spread across the pond.

It was August and the day had been so wet that Mike and I had been resigned to missing a precious day's sport. At teatime, though, the clouds lifted into haze, the rain stopped and it was summer again, Mary said, "Go," and so we went, down to the Saxon Ponds.

I was happy to fish off the dam in the lower pond, setting my stall out for whatever came along. Mike, though, was determined to catch his first carp from the pond and I had left him free-lining a big piece of bread flake as close to the reedbed as he could cast, some ten yards away from him. After an hour, I was lost in the atmosphere of the pond, half-conscious of warmth and birdsong, half-watching a float that moved only occasionally as some fish brushed the line. My reverie was broken by the crack of a pistol shot. No, it was the sound of monofilament snapping under sudden stress. Mike had been broken!

He came down the bank towards me, looking distraught and excited. "Just lost a monster, Pete!" he jerked out. "Snapped me in a second!"

"So I heard," I grinned, to Mike's exasperation no doubt. "Best check your line and try again." Which is what he did, re-tackled and disappeared into the distance once more.

Perhaps half an hour later, I heard a shout for help. When I reached him, he was standing in the shallow water, deep enough though to cover his wellingtons, a fact he seemed unaware of. His rod (my Mark Four Avon, by the way) was well bent, the whining line taut to the reed bed opposite, where the swirls of a well-weeded fish showed he'd latched into a good 'un.

There was nothing I could do but stand beside him and make encouraging comments. Perhaps that helped his patience. Slowly, over what seemed a very long time, he worked the fish out of the reeds and then we knew that it would be ours. The battle, on six-pound line, was a good one, but the carp made no more attempts to seek the reeds and eventually Mike drew the still resisting fish

The Saxon Ponds

over the waiting net, which suddenly seemed small. Fourteen and a half pounds it weighed, a half-tone mirror carp in perfect condition save for a sore patch where a scale had snapped off during the fight, perhaps the result of the reed bed entanglement.

"What a fight and what a beautiful fish," Mike muttered as he squeezed his socks as dry as he could, grinning up at me. "Well worth the trip from the other side of the world."

I agreed.

Over the next few years, the fish grew well and provided increasingly challenging fishing as they became even wiser. Then, in 2011, I found one lying dead on the bank near the sluice, with its shoulder eaten away by an otter. By 2012, all had perished. The last one, our prized 20-pounder, had been carried a hundred yards downstream to a silt trap, where I found the corpse on the bank. Or perhaps it had flopped over the sluice boards to avoid its attacker. I could imagine the terrible struggle. But there it lay, with just one bite out of the throat, a fish that had grown on in my pond for nearly 15 years. What a waste!

The Saxon Ponds

The Saxon Ponds

INTERLUDE

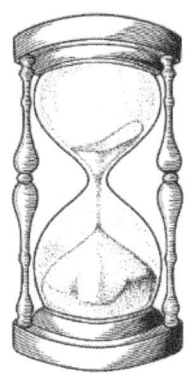

Sad though the demise of my cherished carp was, it led to new opportunities. Carp are splendid fish but they are greedy. Their unplanned absence meant more food for other fish, and I began to manage the two ponds accordingly. The shallower upper one now contained just crucians and tench, with Moby Dick, which fish I'll explain later; the lower pond those two main species plus roach and perch.

The late 1990s and early noughties had seen a resurgence of interest in crucians. I have come to call them this, hoping to persuade others to distinguish them from common carp, with which they had long been confused.

I have told the story elsewhere[1] of the birth and flourishing of the crucian conservation movement. Relevant here is the fact that the Saxon Pond crucians were important to my work on the species that resulted in the publication in 2010 of 'Crock of Gold – Seeking the Crucian Carp' (sic).

Already, by the early 2000s, the upper pond crucians had something of a following. There were many of them, from tiddlers to two-pounders. When the small crucians became too numerous,

---

[1] *One Last Cast* 2019 and *Crucian Renaissance,* by Chris Turnbull, 2021

The Saxon Ponds

we netted them out for sale, with the best always returned or stocked into the lower pond. Angling pressure was low and the crucians and their companion tench were always in sparkling condition.

Influenced by the crucian's rarity, 'names' in the angling world visited or became members. Chris Y., Martin B. and Hugh M. fished and filmed a light-hearted competition for the 'Catching the Impossible' series. Keith A. came with a crew of technicians for his popular radio angling programme.

It was peaceful fishing, but there were moments of drama too, when someone hooked one of our 'manic' tench, strong fish of up to 4lbs that took some holding out of the white water lilies. I had planted these in the upper pond, keeping the beds under control with a scythe on a rope. It became the sort of traditional fishing that was increasingly rare even then and is even more so nowadays.

Things have changed little since those days. The upper pond still has its crucians and tench, though now they have roach and perch as companions, as well as Moby Dick. This is because, since the dredging of the lower pond by the new owner, our fish have been concentrated upstream. Only now the lower pond is maturing are we able to move fish into it. 'Our' pond is still a sensitively controlled wilderness; the wildlife still abundant.

I limit members to fourteen, a number decided on by the available swims in the upper pond. My anglers fish on a flexible rota, so that no more than seven can be there on any one day. Anyone can fish off-rota if there is a free place, straightforward enough in these days of easy communication. Thus, there is little angling pressure. Usually, a member has the pond to himself.

The one complication has been Moby Dick, Jim's name for him or her, the only carp to survive the otter attacks. I ill-advisedly moved this fish to the upper pond during a cropping of the lower pond several years ago. Panic had set in, with far more fish to deal with than I had expected, and there was no time to make special arrangements. Now one carp amongst hundreds of crucians is not

The Saxon Ponds

sensible fishery management but, by a great stroke of luck, Moby Dick appears to have no sexual urges, so hybridisation has not been a problem.

This strange fish has never been caught, despite being visible throughout the summer, lazily cruising from one end of the pond to the other and back again, usually uninterested in angler's baits. Just once or twice, a fisherman has been in contact with a monster that contemptuously breaks the line, but whether this was Moby Dick or one of the big, hard-fighting tench in the pond is beyond our ken.

How big is this elusive fish? The pessimists say six pounds, the wishful thinkers 16 pounds. Perhaps its strangeness goes beyond its behaviour; perhaps it can change its weight at a whim.

And what of the anglers? The D-----d Dabblers I call them. They have been together now for over a decade, with very few changes of membership. Some fish there very seldom but would not dream of giving up their right to be in such a special place. One lives hundreds of miles away and visits Wessex but rarely. Work parties and fish-ins are well supported by a core of the keenest.

We enjoy being an old-fashioned group in other ways than avoiding common carp, well-named in our opinion. Built cane rods are not obligatory but failure to use a centrepin reel does raise eyebrows. Opening day, June 16th, is always looked forward to with great expectation, as you can read in what follows. We are happy to catch small fish as well as big ones. No-one is envious of anyone else: cooperation rather than competition is our password, though fish-ins do breed friendly rivalry. Kelly kettles send up plumes of smoke on many a day after the crucians, or the tench, or the roach.

Let me take you through the next 13 years, to nearly now. Let my anglers describe some of our great fishing times, our social occasions, and some of the problems we've had to deal with.

The Saxon Ponds

The Saxon Ponds

CHAPTER FIVE

The 'Dabblers' Though the Years

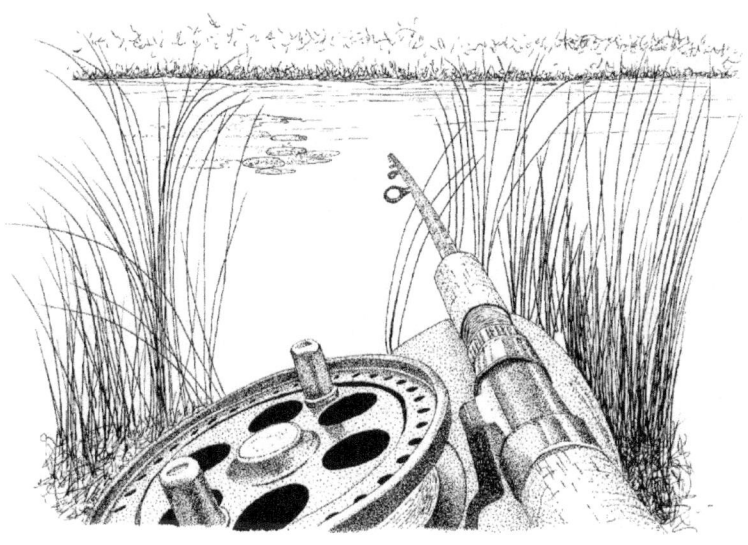

2011 – Nearly Now

June 16th, 2011

The 16th, a ceremony day that one should, if at all possible, celebrate between lily pads with tench. This is of course something of a dream. This high-day's pond is untrammelled, uncivilised even, with no boards, scalpings or gravelcrunch, even the path around the lake is little more than shorter buttercups than those on either side, the whole enclosed in a small green valley. The main concession to mankind is the double sleeper that provides the

The Saxon Ponds

bridge (and I dignify it) across the source of the ponds' life blood at the valley's tip.

"N.'s nicked the first of the best fishable lily swims, quite right too, but made room for me to sashay by his spot. Making a space among the buttercups, I did no more than plonk a fine cane tipped porc. quill by the lilies and wait for something to happen. N. recommended bread so I started with that and a few thin hemp scatters. Very little happened for 20 minutes, except N. showing me a 1¾lb crucian, a wondrous gleaming treasure that didn't deserve so light a weight. I missed a twitch-bob and when P. turned up, doing the rounds, I got a firm, obliging bite and something bolted hard into the pads and pulled out the hook. I was reminded they go hard here.

"After this I caught one, two, then three *Carassius* all about 1lb, small tench plugging the gaps. This continued during the sun's patches, scudding clouds moving too fast for rain until late lunch, then we had the first of the showers that stropped down the valley like a haughty mezzo-soprano making the noise of tearing newspaper. Calm intervals are scented with wood-smoke and damp earth and have the expectancy of fish edging out from the pads' shelter. Crucian arrived in clumps of like size, some hand sized and two stunning fish that went 1½lb and 1lb 10oz. On top of these riches were tench that pulled very hard despite their lack of size, perhaps 1¾lb the largest. After several mini-Sturm-und-Drangs, I missed a sitter, bumped another and then lose a fish in a massive swirl, near carp-like. No mudpigs here though.

"The crucian fight is hard and fast, rattling up the line from the fast tail beat, the carp has a slower beat and a draught-horse pull, the tinca's softer muffled beat coming from the big flexible screws nature provides. A big tinca then, or big for the pond, a reminder that seldom-caught tench fight harder than 'king' carp pound for pound, as hard as a 'wildie'. Crucians are not to be sneezed at, they have a sudden standing-start power and even a 1lb fish races across

The Saxon Ponds

the swim and pushes hard into the pad-stalks. Roach, rudd and perch all slower off the mark and quicker to give in.

"The swim fades and the last bite 40 minutes later gives up another 1lb gold-service plate, I realise that concentration is shredded after five hours of rapt attention to a needle-slim piece of bamboo. I take a stroll about, noting a flower not seen yet, tall, lightweight cow parsley like, mauve flower heads. This, I later find out is Valerian, once and still used as a sedative, possibly the last thing you'd need at this well in reality's surface. There are buttercup petals floating on the pond-surface, gently wavering from the under-squirm, so sated, pack away, stroll about the lower pond and head for some buttered-toast scrambled eggs.

"The best of 16th's, eclipsing a misty dawn on a Stour weir with grayling - I ramble on home along the lanes with Led Zeppelin II and a smile."

So wrote Cole. That demands explanation. First, Cole is Colin, one of four of us that I nicknamed in those days 'the D-----d Dabblers', a name that has stuck. We worked, fished and talked over coffee together in those early years and still do so, given the opportunity.

The numbers of the Dabblers have risen over the years to the 14 men that fish the ponds today, many of them giving up their spare time to do the cutting and mending that even a small fishery demands. We are a mixed and talented crew. There is a famous cinephotographer, a Right Reverend, a learned academic, a brilliant electronics design engineer, two fine craftsmen in wood, two EA stalwarts, a notable book collector, a site manager from the Northeast, a cultivator of plants for shady places, an IT expert, a skilled gardener, a retired project manager in the nuclear industry, and me, the moving spirit.

Cole is my webmaster. Aware of my fascination with crucians and my book, 'Crock of Gold – Seeking the Crucian Carp', he volunteered to devise and maintain a website devoted to the species, a great source of information for everyone interested in the species. Many

The Saxon Ponds

of the descriptions of our activities that follow come from that flourishing website.

Another Dabbler enjoyed the same good Opening Day, Neil, now no longer with us. Rumour has it that he died on a riverbank somewhere. If that is true, it was an appropriate place to go. Neil was one of the most dedicated and successful anglers I have ever known. He wrote thus:

"The weather forecast was not good, but there appeared to be a window around the middle of the day. Just the period when the crucians fed best last season. Any excuse to avoid an early start. The days are long gone when I arose before dawn to cycle two miles to Orpington lakes for three hours fishing before commuting to central London.

"On arrival at the Saxon Ponds, the weather was similar to the final day last season. Cool and breezy with heavy drizzle. Again, my optimism faded. I settled in a sheltered spot between the lilies. Unlike last June, when there were plenty of signs of activity, the surface was only disturbed by the wind. In the circumstances only a very small amount of bait was introduced, before tackling up.

"The tiny black tip of a 2BB float settled down to a no. 6 one inch from a size 12 barbless hook. Now the lilies are up it would be stupid to use a light line, so the hook was tied to 4lb line. Just as well, as the first hour produced six tench, which all fought like tigers, particularly three females around 2lbs 8oz - 3lb. The bites made my delicate set-up pointless.

"I then introduced another small amount of bait and rested the swim while wandering down to the bottom pond to see how our local resident, David, was faring. He caught two lovely small crucians while we talked, an unusual catch there last year. David was already beating me on the crucian front. A benefit from the winter netting of the top pond, when some were moved to the bottom pond. I then baited up a secluded swim on the bottom pond and returned to my original swim. Still no bubbling! Despite that, the crucians were

The Saxon Ponds

feeding but very cautiously. The next hour or so saw twelve beautiful crucians grace my net, all between 12oz and a "weigher" of 1lb 14oz. The float never went under during that whole spell. Several times I found myself instinctively playing a fish but could not recall the bite. Colin arrived during that spell. An even later riser than me! I recommended the other end of the lily beds. then Peter arrived to see how we were all doing. Colin was already catching by then.

"I rested the swim again and tried my baited swim on the bottom pond. In less than an hour it gave me three lovely roach, including a magnificent looking fish of about 1¼lb and four crucians, two were small and the better ones were both about 1lb 8oz. All the fish were in excellent condition. David caught a big tench right in the margins while I was there.

"I returned to the top pond, where Colin was still catching. Both species were still feeding. On catching my thirtieth crucian I packed up, well satisfied. Colin appeared to be enjoying similar success so I left him to it. A very enjoyable day in good company. The sixteenth is still magical in a few rare circumstances!"

Manager's Musings: March 31st, 2012

"Today we netted the Top Pond and re-stocked the Bottom Pond with the best fish. I'd planned to return about 100lbs of fish less than we had removed from the Bottom Pond on 18th February, to allow for growth. Each pond supports 300-400lbs of fish and I use this rough figure as my management guideline. I thought that if I cut down the number of big carp from eight to four and reduced the number of tench, I'd be getting somewhere close to my target. Unfortunately, it didn't quite work out like that, as you'll see.

"For once, because I didn't think we'd have very many surplus fish and wanted to save money, we did the job without the help of our usual professional, Andy. That was mistake number one. Pulling the net round the lake had never seemed very complicated when Andy did it but we had serious difficulties with the mud. So much so that one of our volunteers, who shall be nameless, twice got almost

The Saxon Ponds

immovably stuck. His plaintive cries for help were ignored because we had more important things to do but eventually he got himself out leaving his waders behind him. These were dug out later!

"Surprisingly the first sweep of the net was brilliantly successful - even tiny tench and mussels came in, along with the big carp, some fine tench and roach and thousands of crucians, mostly second year fish of 4"-6" but with a very good number of specimens to over 2lbs. The huge number of fish made things complicated, though.

"I'd taken out three boards (perhaps two would have been wiser) from the sluice to reduce the netting area so the fish were in quite shallow water at the final pull-in. Our first job was to get the roach and perch into the bottom pond as soon as we could because they would have been the first to suffer in the silty, over-crowded conditions. Meanwhile the carp were moved into a floating holding net. Then we concentrated on the crucians and 120 lovely fish to 2lbs or so were carried down to their new home in buckets. Meanwhile, crowds of young crucians and the smallest tench were lifted back into the pond we were netting.

"This left some really splendid tench, many over 3lbs, in the net and I weakened and allowed ten of the best back into the pond and another sixteen down to the bottom pond. Then I panicked a bit at the sight of our carp wallowing in the shallows and decided to put all 8 back down into the Bottom Pond rather than keep 4 in the very shallow water in the Top Pond for later collection.

"So, to cut a long story short, we ended up with putting some 350lbs of fish into the Bottom Pond instead of the 250lbs I'd intended. Learn from my mistakes, friends! This means that I shall need to feed the fish throughout the summer in order to keep them in good condition. Regular feeding can double the capacity of a pond so it shouldn't be a problem apart from giving myself more work. I'll have to buy pellets, too, of course.

"Now, both ponds are full and ready to go for June 16th. The Bottom Pond should produce some fantastic fishing, particularly for the crucians. The Top Pond has mainly small crucians to about 1lb

The Saxon Ponds

with some nice tench and a couple of grass carp and a chub for variety. I may well feed this pond before the planned cropping in the early winter so that we get maximum yield to provide funds for a possible dredging - Cole's experience with the mud has highlighted a need and the pond was last done 10 years ago."

Manager's Musings: 2012/2013, Season Round-Up:
"After what seems like the last 12 months of winter, let's hope that 2013/14 turns out to be a hot and bumper season. When we netted the top pond, in November we found that growth rates have been dismal and that there were very few young fish, all thanks to the ultra-poor summer. Sport was pretty patchy but as you can read below, *some* decent fish were caught. And, of course, the ponds are still a marvellous place to visit to get away from it all.

"We put back all the best crucians and some nice tench after netting the top pond. I think we missed quite a lot of the latter because the results didn't reflect the numbers of tench caught on rod and line during the season. The water was very cold when we did the job and it's quite easy to drag the net over the top of fish hunkering down in the mud. It will be interesting to see what comes out early season. I don't want it to become a tench pond rather than a crucian pond!

"My plan for the top pond is that the crucians will breed well this year but if we missed a lot of tench that becomes less likely. I rely on this pond to provide numerous young crucians to boost the species - so let's hope this summer is warmer and the tench aren't too much of a problem. The fishing for the crucians in this pond will be more difficult because we sold most of the 4" - 8" fish to make room for the (hopefully!) new year's hatch, but there are enough bigger ones there to give you some sport If you're good enough!

"The bottom pond stock remains the same as last season, with numerous good roach, crucians and tench and a few cracking carp. Last year I felt the pond was over-stocked and fed the fish on pellets throughout the closed season and until the end of June. I think on

The Saxon Ponds

reflection that this was a mistake and that the low water temperatures meant that the fish were not eating as keenly as is usual at that time of year. Even in July and onwards, when I'd stopped feeding, sport didn't improve very much and blank days were commoner than they should have been. It may be, of course, that the fish were feeding earlier or later than usual.

"Still, N. had some good fishing, as you can see from his account below. JAA had an interesting 16th, with a beautifully conditioned low-double carp on the split shot he was "using instead of a plummet - there's a pic on his website: Quite an angling feat this, because he was geared up for crucians! (JAA says - .'An Octofloat, 4lb line and a size 14...'). This was the only carp caught during the season. They can often be seen but remain a challenge! Duncan eventually did quite well with the bottom pond crucians by fishing early mornings - those who came later didn't do quite as well. The roach were elusive, though there's now a new generation of good fish coming through and you can often see them rolling during the last hour of daylight. Tench have come out to about 3½lbs from both ponds.

"There have been no signs of otter or cormorant predation but please be vigilant and report any sightings to me.

"We've cut back the rhododendrons and dogwood so that you should find walking round the ponds much easier. JAA and 'The Woodsman' made two big bonfires of the cuttings and we enjoyed old-fashioned spuds baked in foil in the ashes. D. and R. helped with the netting. Thanks to all of them for their willing efforts.

"The top end of the top pond, including the silt trap, has been dredged and that part looks rather muddy at the moment. Hopefully, by the beginning of the season it will have greened up and not look too unsightly, though again we need good weather to help things dry out and for plants to grow. By the time you get this newsletter, the big and dangerous willow at the top of the bottom pond should have been pollarded and the over-hanging dead oak branch cut back. Notices have been displayed by the top pond warning about

The Saxon Ponds

the danger posed by the over-hanging power cables - but of course you wouldn't be fishing near them anyway!

"Realistic targets for the two ponds are as follows. Please let me know if you do any better! You'll notice that these weights are the same as for last year, thanks to our dismal weather: *Bottom Pond*: roach 1lb 4oz; crucians 2lbs; carp 16lbs; tench 3lbs 8oz. *Top Pond*: tench 3lbs 8oz: crucians 1lb.

An occasional guest has been lucky enough to share our little fishery. Here is a report from one such visitor:

July 13th, 2013: Paradise Regained:

"Let me be frank right at the outset, "wrote Nobby. "This isn't a tale of crucians, they were notable for their absence this time, but I didn't have too bad a day and as usual, the Ponds were a lovely place to be in High Summer.

"High Summer means getting up ridiculously early and I deliberately chose a nearby pub that has a back door I could sneak out of at first light for my B&B.

"A short, quiet drive through old villages draped in mist and I was silently letting myself in to The Ponds at 4.45a.m. Tackling up in the half-light chatting quietly to DH, I was going to join him on the Lower Pond when we spotted a lot of tench bubbles fizzing all over the place near the dam wall and I knew I had to cast to them. Why go searching for fish when so many of them were happily advertising their presence?

"A cane rod not fished with since being restored and a newly modified Speedia centrepin made my first few casts a little poor, but on the third I was spot-on amongst the bubbles and followed with a few small offerings to keep them interested. It wasn't long before the float twitched as fish brushed against my line or swirled the bait off the bottom with the wash from their tales and I knew it wouldn't be long...

"The float dipped slightly, came up again and then was gone before I could react. I lifted the rod up as quick as I could and the tip dived for the water and the reel spun in my hand as a fish ploughed across the water to my right. With the rod kicking in my

The Saxon Ponds

hand and the tip taking bigger and bigger plunges down to the water I had to let the fish run-on with the reel burning across my thumb, but eventually it slowed down only to turn and come flying back to the left with me desperately trying to recover line and keep in contact with it. A couple of bats of the reel and I could feel the fish once more just as it turned yet again and ploughed back through the baited area with me now grabbing the spool in both hands to slow it.

"I think the fish and I tired about the same time. He'd probably had a better night's sleep. It was twelve minutes past five and I looked down at a tench of about 3 pounds sitting patiently in the net as I slipped the hook out and put him back without taking him from the net.

"I caught a couple of smaller ones over the next half hour but it soon became clear the tench had moved off after that disturbance. Quite why the tench in the top pond scrap so hard I don't know, but they do and they are a very different fish indeed from those poor, frequently caught individuals who live in more commercial waters. They warrant a trip just to fish for them alone really and whilst one does go to The Ponds for crucians, it's impossible to be disappointed by such fishing.

"As the light increased, I moved to the Lower Pond to join DH and we fished a couple of spots on the South side, generously leaving the more productive side to JAA and GP who were to join us later. Or so we honestly thought.

"Finding any fish proved hard work and the only spell of note during the rest of the morning was an hour where I managed to occasionally hold some perfect roach of just under a pound in my swim. I'm no great roach angler but I did get a bit of a rhythm going for a while and actually managed a half dozen of the quick-biting flighty things before they moved off. Each one, lit up by the mid-morning Sunlight, was a picture of vibrant health and hard to put back so perfect were they to look at.

"DH had a steady day to my right, finding a crucian at last, but poor JAA and GP didn't get a bite. So much for the better swim, sorry...we meant well. At 11.30 a.m. the whole Ponds went quiet and I feared we'd not see another fish before darkness.

The Saxon Ponds

"We called lunchtime early and DH assembled his fiendish folding barbeque and loaded it up with fine charcoal followed by some seriously high-quality sausages as I thawed out the slow-fried onions in my cool box and got bread rolls and sauce bottles out. We know how to live!

"Just as the food was ready we were joined by Peter and DR whose sense of timing was astounding. It was almost too hot to eat now, the temperature hovering around 31°C, and we just quietly nattered in the shade, ate scoldingly hot sausages and watched The Ponds shimmering in the heat. During the whole day I saw two walkers hand in hand and a half dozen light aircraft high above us in the bright blue sky. A perfect Summer's day fishing at The Ponds again. Contentment personified.

"Thank you, DH, for the invitation and thank you, Peter, for once again providing me with the highlight of the year's fishing. Please can I catch a crucian next time?"

***

"PS from JAA: GP and myself fished from near dawn until dusk with only one bite between us on what was probably the hottest day of the year - luckily GP, my guest, had the bite and a fine roach! Good thing there were sausages. The Ponds, especially the Lower Pond, are fishing well this year, but remain early morning waters and as ever, do not respond well to many footfalls on the banks - as it should be of course."

The Saxon Ponds; 2013/2014 Season

As we hoped, the better summer brought better fishing and sport was good, as NH's report shows:

"First visit to the Lower Saxon Pond yesterday quickly redressed all the relative frustrations of last season. Managed fishery pb's for both crucian and roach! Unexpected, but very welcome.

"When I arrived at 7:30am the crucians were spawning all over the bottom pond, under any overhanging bushes. The roach were in close attendance, feeding on the eggs. Some of the fish of both species were surprisingly big. In the event, I resigned myself to some tench fishing, thinking the crucians and roach would be a waste of time. How wrong can you get!

The Saxon Ponds

"The crucians spawned all morning, finally stopping about 1pm. Despite this, I still caught four crucians, best 2lb 4oz and 2lb 1oz, three roach, all over 1lb, best 1lb 12oz and six tench, ranging from 2lb 8oz to 4lb, real quality fishing! The two biggest crus and all the roach did not seem to have spawned yet. They were in exceptional condition. Unlike the big and long old roach of my first two years, they were shorter and much deeper, with a bronze sheen. Beautiful!! Made up for a total roach blank last season.

"I double checked the weights of the biggest roach and crus, deducting the wet mesh, because they were both four ounces better than my previous pb's at the Saxon Ponds. Just for the record. If the roach have spawned, they have made a miraculous recovery. They are only just spawning in some stillwaters down here near home, a record I think.

"I am sure none of this is news to you but could not resist reporting such a significant turnaround from last season."

DR and DH had some good sessions, but JAA did even better, as he describes...
"...the Lower Pond fished its head off today - I rather reluctantly went home as the tench started to feed, it seemed.

"I had 9 roach to 1lb 4oz, 10 crus to 1lb 8oz, 3 tench at 2lb 12oz, 3lb 6oz, 3lb 10oz, 1 perch. Lost 4 fish to hook pulls and missed a dozen bites. Looking at the fins on the roach and crus they've both spawned and there's already small shoals of fry on the pond.

"Saw one carp mooching about that I'd put around 17lb. Oh yes. And we now have a barn owl, wonderful."

April 2nd, 2015: Dave's Report: 2014/2015 Season

"Without exception I always look forward to my trips to the ponds; it's not that I have to make elaborate plans, I am, after all, only twenty minutes away and with a loaf of bread, tin of corn, shoulder bag and ready set up rod I'm fit to go. (No maggots - I ceased using those at least twenty years' ago and fish almost exclusively with bread for most species). And then the first glimpse of the upper pond as one passes down the track - it couldn't be improved. The

The Saxon Ponds

ponds have been kind to me so far this season, especially the lower pond. The roach are exquisite, not a mark on them, plump silver and metallic blue with bright vermilion fins. Not all though. I've had a few which are flatter in the belly and tending towards a brassy colour. They are also quite slimy, in a breamy kind of way.

"My first sorties - I usually go once a week - saw me catching nothing but roach; but what roach they are. Best so far has been 1 - 07 but I've heard of larger ones having been taken. We are surely not too far away from the first two pounder. I do hope it falls to my rod as I have, in fifty years' fishing, yet to catch a roach of that size. Sometimes I've had fish after fish often with many over a pound but where did those early season crucians go? My friends say I should go on the maggot (and get out of bed earlier) but no, I resist the temptation and if the crucians do not like the flake, I usually try corn. But it has been bread that has taken my best two this season, one of 1-14 and a few weeks' later one of exactly two pounds. Both beautifully conditioned fish and boy do they scrap. Speaking of which I have caught the odd tench to about three pounds and they too go like the proverbial clappers.

"Although the lower pond is my favourite, I do have the odd half day on the upper pond but despite the profusion of small crucians I do not normally mange to capture that many. Those I do are perfectly minted little fellows, the best I've had going a fraction less than a pound. Another welcome visitor to my net, and one that took me by surprise has been a golden tench, not since the halcyon days of Whitley Park have I had one of these.

"In conclusion I will briefly mention that I have fished the infant Nadder that skirts the field behind the cow byre. It's tricky but if you can poke your rod through the gaps there's a few fish to be caught. I've had sardine-sized roach and a proper little wild brownie. Real schoolboy stuff and well worth a try."

The year following, 2015/2016, saw excellent fishing, with good crucians, roach and tench pleasing us all. As usual, both ponds were dominated by hand-sized crucians: 20 or 30 in a day was nothing unusual. The upper pond had been dredged, refilled and restocked, and the fish were in impressive condition, though the crucians were

The Saxon Ponds

just failing to make 2lbs. A two-pounder is everyone's target, a fine fish for such small ponds. Opening Day 1996 was as usual a much-looked-forward-to occasion, As Dave R. describes:

June 16th, 2016: Dave Opens the Season
"The rumble of distant thunder accompanied by a heavy but brief shower does nothing to dampen my spirit; there is still within me the excitement of the new season and approaching the ponds down the final curve of the stony track is worth the three months' wait. I park by the barn, noting that the others are here before me. I cast an eye across the pond and spy the mushroom dome of a brolly half hidden behind a bank of yellow iris. It's Garry, recently retired from academia and in the throes of moving house. He's been up since dawn and has tempted a fine tench to open his account. Beyond him I note how quickly April's bank of daffodils has given way to foxglove and hedge parsley.

"I found Cole on the lower pond catching a good many crucians, fishing, as I expected, in the 'armchair' swim. I opted to fish within chatting distance and after half an hour started to catch a few better fish on both bread and corn. Around 1.00pm the bites petered out and all remained quiet until we packed up at 4.00pm. I had five tench between 2-04 and 3-04 and lost a larger one. I also had eight crucians, the two best being both 1-06, two at about a pound and the rest 4 to 8 ounces."

Great fishing, but July brought a problem, an invasion into the lower pond by dozens of cattle that had made their way through a carelessly left-open gate. This would not necessarily have been a disaster, had the banks been firmed by summer heat. Sadly, though, it was the time of the 'monsoon'; heavy and prolonged rain had made the banks soft and muddy. The steers turned it all into a quagmire, and anyone venturing where the cattle had been could easily have ended up in the water, so treacherous had everything become.

The following week, Jim, his wife two sons, with the help of two more Dabblers, Garry and Kevin, had dug drainage ditches and laid boards over the ten yards or so of ruined bank.

The Saxon Ponds

Routine maintenance – or not so routine, as in this case – goes on all the time. Without it, the ponds would quickly become overgrown, the water shaded and made less productive, the paths more like obstacle courses. We do not aim at excessive tidiness, just accessibility while retaining that sense of wildness that we all enjoy.

As an example, the blockwork of the dam – which in about 1985 had been the club's way of dealing with the permanent leaking through the original greensand blocks that I had once spent so long pointing with waterproof mortar – had become increasingly suspect. I had a builder friend cover the blocks with latex-based, waterproof plaster, which looked much better and sealed the wall well.

Less easy to deal with, though, was the recurring leak in the corner of the dam, where concrete and clay met. We spent many hours trying to staunch this, with blocks, clay, plastic, and sawdust, whatever our latest idea was. Always, though, a year later perhaps, I would see the movement of water that meant it was finding its way round the dam once more.

Stemming the leak became as much a routine as clearing paths and pollarding willows. As for the latter, by the lower pond, lining the dam bank like soldiers on sentry duty, were seven golden willows. To preserve their golden splendour, they needed to be cut back to the trunk every other year, a pleasant enough job on a dry, cold winter's day.

It is just as well that we have a willing and able workforce!

Manager's musings: June 1st, 2017: Pre-Season Update

"Thanks to a lot of hard work from a lot of members, the ponds look ready for 16th June, Opening Day. We have opened out the path around both ponds so that access is straightforward but not TOO easy. In the process, more swims are now available on the Semley bank of both ponds. In the top pond, these are by the water lily beds. No one has caught a fish from that bank before, to my knowledge, so these are nearly virgin swims.

"The fallen tree on the bottom pond, by the sluice, has not yet been dealt with. Our tree man won't be there until a little while after the beginning of the season so it will be interesting to see if the fish are using it as a sanctuary.

The Saxon Ponds

"The bridge over the feeder stream at the top of the upper pond was getting a bit ropey so we have made it as secure as possible for the coming season. The leak we discovered near the sluice on the bottom pond has been attended to. It looks a bit "new" at the moment with its shuttering and sawdust but will soon naturalise and blend in with the surroundings.

"The one minor problem remaining is the emergence of reed seedlings in the top pond - a number of green spikes sticking up in the most unlikely places. These will have to be dealt with asap; otherwise they will become established beds and hasten the silting up of the pond. We have plans to remove them before the beginning of the season so watch this space!

"Unusually, there is plenty of soft weed in the top pond and - for the first time for many years - some in the bottom pond too. You'll probably find a weed rake handy to bring along for your fishing. We have made some effort to clear swims but the Canadian pondweed grows very quickly. It is a pest and there is nothing we can do about it except clear our own swims. In the bottom pond, so far it is curly-leafed pondweed, much less invasive.

"As always, it will be very interesting to see how the fish have grown: whether the big tench have reached 5lbs yet; will this be the year of the first 2lb roach; how may and big are the crucians; and will any of the elusive big perch come out of the bottom pond?

"P.S. We've now dealt with the "reeds" in the top pond. When I say "reeds" I mean sedges, which either the birds had distributed or seedlings had spread. I've never known it happen before.

"When I say 'we', I really mean Jim, who heroically ventured forth on his surfboard and gathered up all the stray plants that we could see. Garry, Dave and I helped with banter and sedge spotting."

The Saxon Ponds

The Saxon Ponds

2017 was 'the year of the weed. The upper pond was invaded by Canadian pondweed. We cleared swims heroically. The manager bought an industrial-sized rake with alloy shafts that fitted together a bit like a chimney sweep's brush. That was not a great success. It was quite heavy and difficult to manage on the narrow banks of the pond. An expensive mistake! It now lurks shamefacedly in a garden shed.

The usual swims were kept clear. Courtesy of Garry, a weed rake on a rope was left by the pond so that fishermen could do their own clearing and that worked well enough. I had worries, though, that fish were being confined to the cleared areas, which could lead to multiple re-captures.

In the event this did not seem to happen and the fish stayed in good condition throughout the summers of '17 and '18, after which the Canadian pondweed miraculously declined, to be replaced by much less problematic curly-leafed pondweed and hornwort.

Another worry about the explosion of Canadian pondweed was that although it richly oxygenated the water during the day, the process was reversed during the dark hours, especially when the weed became increasingly festooned with blanket weed. As well, I had known a monk to be blocked by just such a combination of plants, and as a precaution was prompted to fit a makeshift boom across the outflow.

I need not have worried, though. No disasters occurred and if there was any consolation to all this, it was that the dense weed might have given some protection to the fish from the cormorant storm that was about to hit the lower pond.

June 16th, 2017: Opening Day on the Saxon Ponds
A Midsummer's Day Tench by Garry

"At 4 am, the temperature in our garden was 20°C so I knew it was going to be a hot day, and I went to the Saxon Ponds, fishing from about 5 am to 4 pm. A careful analysis of the ponds and conditions guided my choice of swim: the one that would give me most shade

The Saxon Ponds

for the longest time! The 'double' swim on the lower pond. Plenty of fish activity: the carp was enjoying the conditions, a few fish were in front of me, and the odd fish rolled.

"For the first couple of hours it was a fish every cast using maggots, and nothing at all with other baits. The fish were small roach (up to about half a pound) and perch (up to about 5 inches). By 8 am I decided on a rest from the tiddlers, welcome as they were, baited with double caster (conveniently my maggots were turning throughout the day) and sat back to enjoy the pond and the shade.

"One tench was hooked and rapidly shed the hook. So I persisted. After an hour another tench was hooked and landed, much to my surprise and its consternation. It was a long, male tench of 2lb 10oz, which fought strongly, and expressed its indignation in the net by attempting to fight its way out. It was a relief that we both survived the encounter. No more tench, and no bites on corn, bread, or a friend's magic paste. A bite every cast on maggots. I think I must have caught every tiddler in the pond.

"After a welcome visit from Peter at around lunchtime, I carried on fishing, but the pattern remained the same, until around 3 pm when even the tiddlers deserted me, and I left at 4 pm.

"I am the world's worst bird identifier but even I recognized the kingfisher, huge buzzard, and red kite that came to see me not catching crucians. The farmer was making hay while the sun shone, and so did I. It would have been nice to see a crucian or two, but there is always next time."

...by Jim, too:
"For the last decade or so I've struggled to find the right venue for my 'Glorious 16th' celebrations. Each year I looked through the club books, scoured the day ticket waters, and considered the rivers...but I never quite managed to reignite the old sensation of waking early and heading for a quiet rural pond, as I used to do years ago. I know that these days the focus on the 16th has inevitably swung towards the opening of the rivers, but to me it has always been about enjoying a Stillwater in its early summer splendour. Therefore, it was with more than a twinge of renewed

The Saxon Ponds

excitement that I put my tackle into the car and swept off through the countryside for my first ever opening day at the Saxon Ponds.

"On arrival, the ponds looked beautiful and, although by then it was about 6:30, the day still had that calm early morning magic in the air. Of course Garry had done it properly, getting there at first light, and it was no surprise to see him nestled into one of the new swims...he positively drooled when he saw them for the first time!

"Not wanting to ruin his view, I tucked myself into a spot out of his line of sight and set about quietly getting myself sorted out. After having a quick rake around the edge of an overhanging willow, I 'plinked' my float under the trailing branches, then I nestled back to await developments. I'd purposefully set out my stall to catch a tench, and so with a size 12 carrying a nice big chunk of lob tail I suppose it was inevitable that I would only encounter crucians!! So much for small hooks and tiny particle baits!?

"Things were bubbling nicely within half an hour or so, but I blew my first chance, and then proceeded to lose two fish (both crucians) in quite quick succession....good grief.

"Mike arrived and we said a quick hello, before he tackled one of the classic lily pad swims. It was all shaping up nicely. Fish were moving, nudging lilies and generally making themselves known...but now they were being sneaky. Eventually I got one, but the swim then went dead. Out with the rake again, a cracking little gizmo which screws onto the end of a landing net handle, which allowed me to quietly yet effectively stir things up again in the margin. Then I wandered around to see Garry - to rest my swim, and to blag some top-notch cake.

"Eventually I tore myself away from the cake and chatter, and shortly afterwards I even managed to land another pretty little crucian. I think I did have some tench in front of me at one time, the pin-prick bubbles were 'text-book', but no matter how expectantly I hovered my hand over the rod the float simply sat there without moving. I'll be back to try again for a tinca as soon as I can.

"A highlight of the day was a juvenile hobby which left the dragonfly population 'minus two'. It did so with the kind of ruthless efficiency which was quite jaw-dropping, the poor dragonflies didn't

The Saxon Ponds

have a clue what was happening until it was way too late...and it did all this while your back was turned Peter!

"I had to pack up at around 4 o'clock, but I left with a very happy soul."

That summer, the lower pond fishing was poor, and the reason was clear. The preceding winter had seen an influx of 'the black plague', cormorants. Often, when I was walking down the track on my twice weekly tours of inspection, I would see one or more of the wretched creatures perched at the top of one of the high trees framing the lower pond, and the ground beneath was increasingly filthy with their guano.

This was a management problem of mammoth proportions. It was possible that the fishing on both ponds, not just the lower one, could be destroyed by cormorants, as the carp fishing of the past had been by otters. Most thinking anglers in small waters detest these sea-going birds for their ability to denude a pond of its fish. Herons, kingfishers, grebes and egrets are an acceptable part of the pond's ecology: they predate selectively, and they have a natural place in the food chain. The cormorant, though, is an intruder from the maritime world, as out of place as a seal in a garden pond. Their adverse effect upon biodiversity is enormous.

So what could we do? Shooting the birds was out of the question for many reasons, so we must try to protect the fish in other ways. Our first task must be to make the upper pond as cormorant-proof as possible, because it would have to accommodate the fish from the lower pond while we took measure to safeguard them in their home. Its shape, unlike that of the lower pond, enabled us to put ropes across, with shiny compact discs that twinkled brightly in sunlight and the slightest breeze. We hoped that these measures would at least deter the cormorants and send them elsewhere, at the same time posing no other risks to ducks and other birds.

I found a source of white synthetic rope and bought two 100m reels. On the day of the installation, Nigel cast an easy-to-follow hookless spoon to the far bank, expertly using his marsheer rod and reel for propulsion. 'Easy to follow' was important: we did not need

The Saxon Ponds

an accident from a flying lead. The crew on the far bank attached the rope's end to the line, it was winched back and attached to one of the stakes we had already put in place every five paces along both banks.

Received wisdom at that time was that an overgrown pool was less likely to be predated than an open one. Our experience was the opposite. It was the tree-surrounded lower pond that the birds had attacked, probably feeling more secure there. The more open upper pond, with the proximity of a footpath, had so far escaped their depredations. We wanted to keep it that way.

The scale of what had happened to the lower pond became clear when we netted it in the winter, as I described to the members on the website.

December 3rd, 2017: Manager's Musings

"Hi, everyone. I thought I'd report on the less-than-good netting last Sunday.

"The crucians have been plundered by cormorants and we found only about 20 left, several with horrible gashes on them, though fish vitality being what it is they will probably recover well enough to breed next year. We moved them up to the top pond, where the weed and the ropes will hopefully keep the BP away. About 20 nice tench went up as well, fish to 3lbs or so, together with 1200 roach, mostly 4" - 5" but with some younger fish and some really nice specimens amongst them. The small perch - no big ones turned up - were left in the bottom pond for the herons and the egrets - there were four of them in the water yesterday. I won't repeat the perch experiment...

"While the bottom lake is drained we can install unobtrusive fish refuges against cormorants, so that we shouldn't suffer the same level of predation again. Then we'll re-fill the lake and leave it to mature over the summer, with some gradual re-stocking of roach, crucians and smaller tench from the upper pond via rod and line sessions rather than a big re-stocking via the net. I want to leave

The Saxon Ponds

the fishing in the top lake as good as possible for the coming season, so all the bigger fish will stay in there for the time being. I hope that eventually the EA will let us have a few hundred crucians from Calverton."

David found a source of chestnut paling on the internet and Nigel collected it from the supplier in Kent. With lower pond now drained, we had easy access to those places where we thought sanctuaries would be effective, those with overhead cover from bushes and overhanging trees. The usual core of enthusiasts spent two long sessions installing our refuges and with the pond re-filled, we felt that we had done what we could and that re-stocking could begin, as it did throughout the summer of 2018. Eventually, some 350 fish were moved, crucians and roach. The manager saw them in two big shoals one bright September afternoon. The fish looked to have grown and to be in fine condition.

In the autumn, Leigh improvised an underwater camera from his mobile phone, some plastic waterproofing of limited efficiency plus his landing net pole. Eureka! The crucians at least were using the refuges, as we could make out from the faint but exciting images on screen. The fish had at least some protection from the expected winter onslaught, a sense of comfort that proved illusory.

The upper pond remained almost free of cormorants that winter. Whether that was because of our ropes and discs or because of the relatively openness of the pond and its proximity to a footpath, I would not care to say. I had a trail camera in operation there throughout the winter and only once was there a shot of a cormorant. I kept my fingers firmly crossed.

The lower pond, though, still attracted the birds. We could do nothing but hope that some of our fish survived in our refuges, that both species had spawned during the summer of respite from predation, and that if the cormorants ate all the bigger fish that would still leave the fry to grow on.

In the meantime, our fishing relied upon the upper pond.

The Saxon Ponds

The Saxon Ponds

June 16th, 2018: JAA's Opening Day

"At 4am, I wasn't overly mithered, but did it anyway. Coffee (pre-loaded pot), eggs (fried) and toast, front-door, car-door. I wasn't first, Garry was already tackling up on the north bank and we quietly shouted greetings. I tackled up with my lucky crucian float and the soft-tipped GTI float rod, built a twelve-month back and racked since. I caught a crucian ten minutes later, then a couple more, this burst of auspiciousness correctly predicting the day's course and I continued to catch steadily in the grey light, mud-coloured water and occasional patches of bubbles. The first four fish helped me to understand I'd missed a ring on the top section, so I was obliged to unclip the float, re-thread...you know the drill.

"A very solid crucian in the 'a bit less than 2lb' category came to hand, really testing the rod's fine tip. Ten minutes later one of the long, lean, 2½lb swim-trashing machines came out, not without some entertaining moments. I nipped out another small one, watched the apologetic sun rise then had another nerve- and weed-shredding big crucian. I opted to amble around, via a fine foxglove, to see how Garry was faring.

"Garry was good enough to lend me his 'guest seat' and while he'd had activity, even a bite as I watched, his day was thus far slower than mine. Jim turned up at 8:45am (ish) and was rebuked for his sloth. Hands were shaken, Jim went off to fish and I left Garry to it shortly thereafter and returned to my seat. Sport remained steady, with two large tench mid-morning and another thumping crucian, perhaps a shade larger than the previous. 'Steady'; that is, as I said to Pete when he arrived with a bucket for any spare roach and small crus; "The right rate to ensure you become tired from fishing before you are tired of the fish." Peter went on, pausing only to move a few crus and roach to the bottom pond (sprat-sized roach were ever-present).

"At noon(ish) Jim called 'lunch-time' and he, Garry and I drank kettle-tea and munched shortbread biscuits. We quickly worked out Garry's cunning scheme, to wit, bringing a 'half-kettle' capacity

The Saxon Ponds

mug, so to ensure tea for all, his cup was filled last...all had caught so all was well and good.

"I pondered calling it a day, grimy eyes, the hay-fever medication wearing off, 4am is feckin' early. However, despite looking less active the swim produced another string of crucians, another large one, then another, the last arriving as Jim came by, *pour encourager les pêcheurs*.

"This last 'biggun', determined to visit all four corners at full pelt, trashed the swim somewhat, so I wandered up to chat with Jim and we fixed many of the world's problems (you should see some improvement by Tuesday lunch-time). Garry went on around that time and although I fished for a little longer, my concentration had fled. So I bade Jim farewell and pottered off for an apposite fish-finger sandwich and a Talisker. And sleep.

"Fine place, fine company, fine day. Very fine."

Summer, 2019: In Search of the Mirror Carp.

First, Cole:

"The plan was to capture the carp. At 4pm it's still 30°C in the shade and I tackle-up behind a handy bush, as it was lurking not 10 yards from the dam. By the time I'd done, it had scooted off to some lilies against the dam wall. I sneak round and lower bread. This fails and it mooches further down the wall. I cast over the fish and it obligingly sidles up and sucks at the bread; when I strike the bread remains...the fish pops up further out, in no hurry...so I sit quietly on the wall for some time, with sweat running down my back, waiting fruitlessly for another opportunity.

"I head for one of the lily-pad swims, wait for the carp to arrive and when it does, a vortex on the far side of this patch, I cast over, see the big tangle and move too much to deal with it. That was that.

"I thread back between the shadows to the car and go through a familiar re-stowing routine. The lizard-brain doesn't like the barn's sepulchral creaks and groans and urges me to shine a light into the

The Saxon Ponds

dark shadows at the back. The more evolved brain knows it's sheep scratching themselves on the far side. I consign the barn-sprites to the pit of rationalism, but muscles on my back crawl as I get into the car. Outside the double-gates I slip the boots off, a relief, and head for home."

Now, Jim:

"I had an unexpected few hours free on Sunday evening, and so I grabbed the chance to fish the top pond.

"Rob had arrived just before me, and he quickly settled into catching steadily on maggots – roach, smaller crucians, and a couple of real clunkers came his way. He was clearly enjoying himself.

"In contrast, things were slow on my side of the pond. I'd set myself up under the shelter of the big oak (it rained briefly as I tackled up), and I fished next to the little overhanging willow between the reeds and lily-pads. I didn't take any maggots, and so I raked the swim and put in a bit of groundbait – then squeezed a bit of stinky paste around the hook and sat back to await events.

"The fizzing and bubbling started quite quickly, and then the float started giving the odd indication that there were fish in the swim. But I'd set myself up with a fairly crude 'lift-method' rig, and so I sat on my hands and waited for a proper bite.

"For some reason, I had chosen to use my childhood float rod rather than the cane 'Kennet Perfection' which has been my weapon of choice at Donhead since the season began. This was a Shakespeare 'Radial Carbon' – a real throw-back to the first generations of carbon rods, which over time has grown to have a rather pleasing retro charm. It's the perfect rod for crucians and 'pond-sized' tench, and so I was perfectly confident that it would (as it has done in the past) happily handle anything the top pond could throw at it.

"The fizzing and bubbling slowly subsided, and still without a fish, I was starting to think about throwing in a bit more groundbait, but

The Saxon Ponds

then, in text-book style, the float smoothly rose up out of the water, pausing momentarily at the point of balance, before falling flat on the surface.

"I'm afraid I wasn't patient enough to wait for the final sliding away, instead I lifted the rod smartly upwards and set the hook.

"It was really at this point that things got a bit weird...the three or four feet of line beyond the rod tip were obviously taken up on the strike, but unlike the hoped for 'lively yet firm' resistance, there was a solid weight which was totally static.

"I lifted the rod a bit more, but rather than anything giving way, the rod simply bent further towards the handle and made no impression on what I'd snagged at all.

"Unbeknownst to me, the creature on the other end of the line was also pondering the situation, and it came to the correct conclusion half a moment before I did.

"I was just starting to think that I'd maybe hooked the bottom when the entire swim exploded. The area of water between the pads and reeds bulged up in a big dome of water, and lines of waves marched out into the pond away from the epicentre. The one and only 'Moby Dick' plunged into the bed of lilies to my left, lifting them upwards on the crest of an impressive bow-wave, before turning right and bolting out into the middle of the pond.

"The 5lb Maxima line graunched around the plant stems, and my poor old rod (which wasn't designed to cope with this type of onslaught when it was brand new, let alone 35 years later), bent like a twig. I still don't know how it remained in one piece. The line tore off again as the fish made a second run, burning my thumb on the paint-chipped rim of the Speedia centrepin, before a swirling heavy splosh way out in the middle of the pond heralded the end of our brief encounter.

"By this point Rob's head was poking over the bush on the far side of the pond, and with a rather startled look on his face he simply said 'I saw the splash'.

The Saxon Ponds

"I retrieved my tackle – minus the last two inches of 4.5lb hook-length, which had snapped at the point my single shot had been pinched above the hook. I was especially pleased to get my float back – I'd only just made it, and this was its first time in the water. Next time it will be attached to 12lb line and a much sturdier rod!

"That 'slack line winding in of shame' is always a strange sensation, the feelings of shock and disappointment mixed with excitement and wonder after an event like that are a heady cocktail. My thumb was stinging, and the water was still gently rocking across the entire pond as I miraculously recovered. So there it is, gents, Moby Dick 1, Jim 0...but it proves that he/she will take a bait, and as the former governor of California would say – 'I'll be back'!

"Hopefully the barbless hook won't have bothered him/her for long, and I hope I've not wised it up too much ahead of collective future efforts to repeat the scenario – except with the right tackle in hand hopefully. I did wonder if maybe the cane rod would have fared any better, or maybe fate protected it from a grizzly splintered death – I'll never know. So there is the challenge, folks – who's next?"

July 7th, 2020: Manager's Musings

"In the spring I was quite negative about the prospects for the summer's fishing. On my visits through the winter, I'd seen cormorants, usually two but sometimes more, on the lower pond. Once or twice I spotted them in the trees on the Donhead bank, wings out to dry. The ground was often covered in guano so I knew they were eating our fish – and there was nothing I could do about it, except hope that some fish were surviving in our refuges.

"Once I frightened two birds off the top pond. Another time I saw a huge disturbance of fish where they were trying to find shelter in the sedges. One day on the top pond I found a nice crucian in a puddle on the bank, where it had jumped out of the water to escape.

"There was no sign of fish anywhere during April and very little in May and I feared the worst. But I was unduly pessimistic and in fact the fishing in the top pond from the beginning of the season has been very good. Cole has been the main beneficiary so far and has

The Saxon Ponds

done very well, with tench to nearly 5lbs, a stunning 2lbs 2oz roach and crucians to about 1lb 12oz, with plenty of small ones as well, including just a few perch. If you go the Cole's website you can see photos of his catches: http://www.anotherangler.net

"The only other reports I've had have been from Duncan, who's had some nice crucians to over 1lb. If you've fished, please let us all know your successes and failures, to help build up a picture of what is happening there.

"Things are not so good on the lower pond. The level is steadily dropping because of the leak. Nigel has some clay which might stop the flow once we can be certain how far down the bank it is. But until them we can only wait and see. Getting a work party together in these Covid 19 days is obviously not straightforward and we may have to leave this to contractors – to do it properly is a major job needing machinery.

"I've only once seen signs of fish in that pond and there's no way of knowing how many have survived. I was unduly pessimistic about the top pond so perhaps I'm wrong about the lower one. If anyone fancies a challenge, how about fishing there?

"I don't yet know what landscaping is planned for the lower pond. If it's going to be dredged and generally altered, we'll need to think about how best to rescue the any fish that remain and put them into the top pond temporarily. We can re-stock later and it may be that contractor activity will keep the wretched birds away this coming winter. The ropes obviously worked to some degree on the top pond so we'll have to do the same again at the end of the season.

"There's plenty of weed in both ponds and you may need to use the rake that's kept at the top end of the top pond, though up to now the actual swims have been pretty clear.

"Moby Dick still swims up and down. If anyone can explain his/her behaviour, please let me know. I have seen him/her feeding on, presumably, larvae on weed stems and leaves but he's shown little interest in baits. Perhaps a fly rod and a Wickham's Fancy or a nymph? Jim? Nigel? Steve?

"The paths are getting pretty overgrown so anything you can do to improve access will be welcome. But, whatever, enjoy the ponds and the wildlife while summer lasts.

The Saxon Ponds

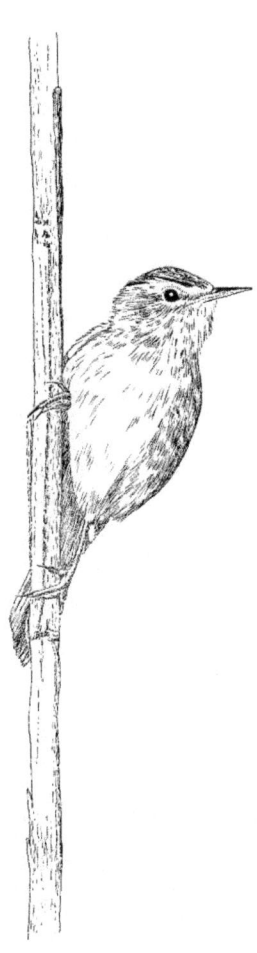

The Saxon Ponds

August 8th, 2020: The Manager Fished the Upper Pond

"After encouraging everyone to send in reports about the fishing – not with very much response, I might add! – I'd better step up to the plate myself.

"For once I treated myself to a good, long session – over five hours, the longest in living memory. Chose to go early afternoon and fish till supper time. Not a good choice, too late to begin and too early to finish.

"I fished for bites with maggots in Jim's swim, because like him I like to overlook the pond. I fed in a small amount of crumb and micro-pellet and waited for the bubbles, which appeared now and then but with no enthusiasm.

"To start with I had no crucians, just the occasional small roach and a little perch – after losing three fish thanks to a defective hook. Out of the blue, late afternoon, I had a nice crucian of about a pound and a half, which had lost its top lip (that's a shame). Then a half-decent roach and a smaller crucian. By the time I came to pack up the swim was just coming to life, with plenty of lily movement and bubbling. I'd have had a shedful if I'd stayed, of course! I lost one fish that charged for the lilies, possibly a tench, but the hook pulled.

"Plusses were plentiful. I had a horrendous tangle, which with patience I managed to sort out so I can still do that. All the fish were in good condition. The weed is in decline except in the third of the pond nearest the dam. I was strafed by a dozen swallows. The moorhen family were busy but not a nuisance. I saw and heard a buzzard. I had no problems with Jim's crayfish. The sun shone just enough and the pond is a wonderful place to be. There are small fish in good numbers but not enough to be a pain. Dave from the landscaping team came to chat and told me they were thinking of moving the sluice back towards the house on the bottom pond, with a proper winding mechanism - wow! Perhaps the promised dredging this winter. There'll be a site meeting 'soon', me included.

"Minuses – none, except I should have stayed on to catch some crus. Oh, and I didn't see Moby Dick, though a crucian, perhaps the one Duncan reported, was surface feeding in the margins in front of me – picking up the habit from big cousin, perhaps. I do suspect

The Saxon Ponds

that the cormorants thinned out our big crucians but that there are some left to challenge you.

"The lower pond level is very low. Dave told me that one of his guys went in in chest waders and could feel fish (eels, he said, though I'd be surprised) brushing up against him, so...

"...the plan is to let out all the water come the autumn and try to catch the fish at the sluice. We'll then move them up into the top pond, protect it with the ropes as usual, perhaps augmented. If there is work on the lower pond that should help deter the cormorants.

"Angling conclusions? Well, we know there are plenty of fish there from early season catches. I imagine that early morning and later afternoon/evening sessions would be best, but who can tell!

"In a fishery that relies on nature rather than artificial stocking, there are always highs and lows. Experience tells me that the good times will return and that increased activity should deter the darn birds. I foresee good fishing for crucians, roach and perch (!), and of course our big tench, in the top pond and cherry-on-the-top-of-the-cake fishing in the lower pond when all the necessary work has been done. My licence gives us the right to fish down there though I would always respect The Landlady's wish for privacy when she is in residence. We can re-stock the lower pond from the top one, I have no doubt.

"My conclusion is that in such a rich pond the angling is a challenge, that there are plenty of fish there and that I'm already looking forward to the next time.

"Your reports to follow, I hope, even nil returns."

March 30th, 2021: Cole's End of Season

"The plan was to try and catch something (anything) at the tail end of the season. Pete had tried manfully, if not fruitfully, to catch from the lower pond, something he'd abandoned in favour of lunch by the time I pootle up. There is little evidence of fish in the lower pond and it is too weedy to net, so it looks as if opening the sluice and catching the fish en passant might be the only option. Hm. We talk

The Saxon Ponds

of this and that; at least 'lockdown' has eased so we might have an actual work-party, as opposed to 'work-pairs'.

"Pete opts to have another go and I opt for the sun on the South bank, a triumph of optimism and warm weather over common sense. Maggots, hemp-seed, a size 16 and a mere 10mm of thin cane peeking from the surface tension; I had expected it to be slow. It is...

"...although I recover from my own idée fixe in time to tweak the hook into a roach which obligingly nips of with two red maggots. Aha. Honour satisfied I take stock of the surroundings and a few pictures, and in this way miss a bite that results in a solid nick. This feels larger but one cannot know for sure...

"...after some time passes I change the maggots for a pinch of bread. Sensibly (I know...) I hold the rod, and as a result, the sudden subsidence of the tip didn't catch me unaware, well not completely; something solid beetles about in a manner that might have been awkward in the summers' lilies, but today is a pleasing minor inconvenience. A crucian, a surprise, but no less welcome for that...

"...I was still clutching said rod when Pete arrived at 4pm-ish, and he, having met with the same success as in his pre-prandial session, opted, in view of the evidence, to fish a little along the bank. Thus it was, we both spend the next 90 minutes catching nothing at the same time...interrupted by the stockman arriving to return some errant sheep from the yard back into the meadow...the sun shines, things buzz pleasantly by, startled awake bumblebees mooching about and a convention of toads in the left-hand reed bed generating fish-like ripples and a continual series of convivial 'quark-quark' sounds. In our favour insects are hatching, occasional bursts of 4-5 emergers which hints at the warming waters (9.4°C) and lengthening days, all of which suggests fish are well advised to be abroad.

"Sometime around 6-ish, Pete starts 'last casts' and my float tip starts on a long series of tiny movements which results in several

The Saxon Ponds

optimistic strikes and exactly no fish. Naturally, as Pete's valedictory car clears the gate, my float zips under. Naturally I miss. The next hour is punctuated by a roach that took the bait 'on the drop', a crow chasing a squirrel with predatory intent (the crow was finally foxed when the quarry ran vertically down an ivy'd oak-trunk) and a series of bites that barely qualified as such. Rum.

"The distant church bells announce '7', I nick off another roach, then a second, then catch two in quick succession, which is why after the next strike when the rod yanks hard around, I realise my fingers had stiffened with cold. The cause gallops off under the left-hand ropes and then, chastened by the warming effect of the reel-rim on my thumb, decides it prefers the dogwood branches, obliging me to stand and move hard right. Ms. Tench now zips off the other way. This repeats for a few diminishing cycles, and so I net a fine lean tench. Heh.

"Now nearing half-light and the air smells of the damp descending the little valley, so I commence last casts and land a nice roach, an actual 'netter', then 'call it' when the first bat swerves to investigate my mid-cast float. Chilly by now, my fingers could do with loosening somewhat to tackle down.

"I've had worst days mid-summer. I put on some 'Good Times Bad Times' and, dodging a barn owl at the bottom of Donhead Hollow, pootle back."

2021: Pre-Season, 2021

"I could have called this 'after the pandemic', except that I guess it'll be with us for a while yet. But what a pleasure it was to see everyone again in more relaxed circumstances at last.

"The Pond is now ready for the glorious 16th, apart from a little last-minute tidying, scheduled for next week. The anti-cormorant ropes have been removed, dogwoods cut back so that they no longer push us into the pond, wet patches in the path stoned and wood-chip covered, two well-worn swims made good in the same way, with smart boards giving a good edge. The fallen willow in 'Jim's

The Saxon Ponds

Swim' has been removed and the swim itself raked to make it clear of debris. The Semley bank path has been cut and cleared, to give access to the tasty swims on that side.

"And the fish greeted us on a cloudy, still and warm morning, bubbling, priming and twitching the water lilies in time-honoured fashion. If you search the huge heap of composting wood chippings in the yard, you can even find the bait to catch them with, lovely little gilt tail worms in good numbers.

"None of this would have been possible without the hard work of Cole, Steve, Robin, Duncan and son Harry. It was a morning to remember, with results that we'll enjoy throughout the summer, I'm sure."

June 16th, 2021: Jim's Opening Day

"I thought I'd let you know how I got on during my opening day session on the top pond.

"Slightly later than planned, I arrived at the ponds at around five o'clock, and although I'd hoped to be there in time to say hello to Cole, I must admit that I was quietly delighted to discover that I had the whole place to myself (no offense Cole, it would have been lovely to see you). No doubt he'd already had his own opening day adventure earlier on.

"I had fully intended to fish in a less familiar spot, but the oak tree seemed to welcome me back with open branches and was providing a lovely area of shade which seemed even more appealing on a day which was a humid 26 degrees. Plus, that view down the pond gets me every time.

"So, I settled into the old routine and was soon drinking tea and eating pork pie while watching the fizzing increase over the lumps of groundbait which I'd thrown into the swim next to the lily pads. After baiting the hook with maggots, I swung the little peacock float into place and settled back in my chair.

The Saxon Ponds

"A squirrel in the branches above me caught my attention, and as I looked back at my float the line was rising smartly and the float was well and truly 'gone'. A pristine little perch was the result, scoffing as it had the bait deep into its mouth – a timely reminder why we use barbless hooks. A gentle probe with the disgorger soon did the trick, no harm done.

"It's nice to get lots of bites on opening day, and so I stuck with maggots and caught more perch along with some perfect little roach, crucians and 'bars of soap' tench – the next generation of all species seem to be present in abundance.

"I suppose the chance was always there that a bigger fish would come along, and so it did in the form of a lovely tench. It went into the net after a decent scrap, and really made my day. More small fish followed, and then an unremarkable bite resulted in a jarring wake-up call as a very strong fish bolted at high speed into the lily pads, presumably a good tench. The Kennet Perfection barely got a chance to offer an opinion, and as the line fell slack I knew that not only had I caught my first fish of the season but I'd also been 'duffed-up' for the first time too.

"Regardless of Moby Dick (who was charging around the pond, in spawning mood I suspect), I think the tench warrant increasingly stout tackle nowadays as they continue to grow and thrive in the food-rich pond. I retackled, licking my wounds, thankful to have only lost the last inch or two of my rig - another reminder about those barbless hooks. Hopefully the fish which beat me wasn't burdened by it for very long.

"More smaller fish came to the net, and the heavy rain which had been forecast stayed away as the light dipped and the day started to turn into night. A text-book bite resulted in a heavy and more ponderous resistance, and a proper to-ing and fro-ing ensued. I thought the fish was coming around to my way of thinking but a last-second lunging change of direction scuppered me. The fish did that amazing magic trick that they sometimes do, and neatly transferred the hook to one of the lily stems.

The Saxon Ponds

"I have a feeling that was a good crucian, and I must admit that I was a bit disappointed that I didn't get to meet it properly. Thankfully I got all my tackle back this time.

"But no time for despair, the swim had erupted with fizzing and the slow progress of feeding 'fish' around the swim was easy to chart by their trails of bubbles on the surface. It wasn't long until the float dipped and slid oddly to the side. There was resistance as I lifted the rod, but not the right type. A black and rattling crayfish came clattering to the net, hooked as it turned out in its tail, reason number three for favouring those barbless hooks! It is a 'non-native invasive species' and I felt obliged to do the right thing and killed the poor thing with the heel of my boot, hopefully Mr Fox found it during the night so its flesh didn't go to waste.

"The swim produced a few more small fish (tench, crucians and roach) but as the church clock chimed ten times the bats came out to hunt, and I called it a day. I let my eyes adjust to the low light and drank more tea as I slowly packed away my things. Back at the car the darkness had properly arrived and as I drove up the track I thought how lucky we are to have access to such a wonderful little lake.

"As I turned out onto the lane the first heavy raindrops landed on the windscreen, it rained steadily all the way home. I dropped the car windows and drank in the petrichor..."

June 29th, 2021: Manager's Musings

"I don't go fishing very much and when I do, it's usually to check on the condition of the fish or to meet up with a pal. Tuesday, though, I just felt like an hour or three by the water for fun.

"It didn't start too well. I'd meant to be at the Saxon Ponds by 10am but had forgotten about the one-day closure of St Bartholomew's Street. In fact the blockage was well beyond the turn-off down the track to the ponds but I took the 'Road Closed' notice too literally and followed other routes. No use! When I

The Saxon Ponds

eventually ignored the notice and found my way to the ponds, it was nearing 11 o'clock.

"Not that it mattered very much. The fish were slow to feed and, just as I used to find on the Victorian Estate Lakes, it was between 12 and 2 when the fish turned on. Anyway, I had time to get comfortable in my specimen-hunter's chair after digging the dung heap for a handful of lively little red worms and tackling up.

"I chose Jim's Swim, because there's plenty of room for bucket and haversack, and a nice easy cast to the edge of the water lilies. Perhaps I should have raked. The pondweed is spreading and once or twice was a nuisance. Hugh always raked before he fished there and his catches were often memorable.

"Anyway, I didn't. Instead I ground-baited with a sweet 'bream and skimmer' mix laced with some micro pellets and waited for the fish to arrive, which they were slow to do. I had a couple of little perch and a slightly bigger roach. Then all went quiet apart from some slow, oh-so-slow 'unmissable' bites that I just could not hit. They said "crayfish" to me, but only Jim can actually catch them.

"I tried close in, just under the rod tip, with not much result; then I tried the far edge of the lilies, enjoying the challenge of casting well out using a centre-pin. The float vanished and before I could gather my senses a monster had taken the line into the water lilies and I'd lost a hook! One-nil to the tench. My, they do pull!

"By about 12.30 the bubbling became more organised and suddenly I was catching fish – fat, deep, hand-sized crucians in spanking condition. Then came a hectic battle with a big tench, a female of about 3lbs, really thick and solid when I unhooked it in the landing net, using my brand-new medical forceps. Fingers get stiff over a certain age and tench lips are rubbery and hold a hook well, as you know, so I was glad of assistance.

"There were some roach as well, nothing much over 4oz but handsome fish. Three smaller tench too, up to half a pound or so. Very promising. And I think I hooked Moby Dick! A whale took line at express pace way across the pond, with a great swirl in the pondweed many yards away. Wow! Hook number two lost.

The Saxon Ponds

"At 2.15 I packed up, already a bit later than I'd promised. It's great to have all the gates open, with easy parking. Once the grass has been cut and the sheep let loose on those first fields we'll have probably three gates to negotiate.

"Conclusions? There are plenty of fish, as we've all found, some good ones amongst them. No need yet for any supplementary feeding, though that may come next month. And we'll have lots of roach, tench and crucians for the lower pond when we net in the winter – though there's much to do down there yet and things don't always go exactly as planned.

"I didn't catch any bigger crucians, though others have. And there has been as yet no sign of the big roach and perch that we caught last season. All the crucians were pukka, with no sign of hybridisation, so perhaps Moby Dick is an 'it'".

July 15th, 2021: Manager's Musings

"I've started to give the fish some supplementary food – organic wheat, soaked for at least 48 hours, not huge quantities, just 5lbs or so dry weight every two to three days. I feel that it's time to do it now the first flush of natural food is over.

"I always worry a bit about this. How quickly will the fish take to the new diet? Will feeding make them more difficult to catch? Will it make any noticeable difference to their condition?

"So I went fishing yesterday to see what I could find out. I had the pleasure of Cole's company and no doubt he'll be writing a report for his website.

"As usual I took a fork for the worms in the beautifully decomposing dung heap and as usual found catching red worms almost as much fun as trying to catch fish. I took some soaked wheat out of the bin as a change bait, though it proved a bit too hard still.

"I fished in the second boarded swim on the south (Donhead) side of the pond, leaving 'Land's End' for Cole. The pondweed is spreading but the swims remain pretty clear so I didn't have to rake. I put in a little of my currently favourite groundbait – a sweet concoction meant for bream, mixed with some 'Frenzied Hemp' and

The Saxon Ponds

a few micro-pellets. I'm not sure that it made any difference. I used worm on a size 12 hook.

"The fishing was a bit slow until about 6pm, when I had a nice crucian getting on for one-and-a-half pounds, followed by a scrappy half-pounder in great condition. From then on, the fish came regularly, every ten minutes or so: mostly hand-sized crucians but with three young tench amongst them. Nothing to match Cole's big, fat tench of over 3lbs, though.

"Conclusions? Well, there are a lot of fish there, to judge from all the activity – the water was never still, despite the lack of wind. So I'll carry on feeding. The fish were in supreme condition and still hungry enough to bite pretty well, though they were never crawling up the rod.

"It was a delight to be beside the pond for four hours or so on a warm, still summer's evening, listening to blackbirds, thrushes and chiff-chaffs – a pleasure I can still just enjoy despite worsening hearing. And, of course, catching enough fish.

"Please email us all how you get on down there and the condition of the fish that you catch, because that will help me decide whether to increase or decrease the rate of feed. It's a good thing to have plenty of fish because we shall need to re-stock the lower pond when the time is right.

"You'll notice how high-backed the smaller crucians are, while the biggest are less bream-shaped. Perhaps that has something to do with the perch in the pond or perhaps the biggest crucians are having to compete with big numbers of smaller young ones and need more food. When we sort out the fish for the two ponds, this is something we can address.

"The grass in the meadow has not yet been cut and access is straightforward, with no gates to open and shut. This may change sometime soon, with good weather forecast."

July 26th, 2021: Social Fishing

"Monday 26th was a day to look forward to for the Manager, Jim, and guests Hugh and Trevor. The weather seemed to be playing its part too, with warm sunshine, a gentle breeze and just enough cloud – though it had a trick up its sleeve for later, as you'll see.

The Saxon Ponds

"We met up by the barn at about nine o'clock, touched elbows and grinned at each other. The Manager had elected not to fish but had come just to chat, encourage and sympathise as was appropriate, perhaps to take a few photos, though typically he'd left the memory card in the computer at home and so was limited to about a dozen. No matter – we had plenty of photographers.

"Hugh had started a bit earlier and greeted us with a complaint that the fish in the pond were too big, having briefly contacted one of our tench in the 'Land's End' swim. Not allowed to use his beloved pole because of the incredibly strict rules of the Saxon Pond fishery, he'd come as close to cheating as he could by using a state-of-the-art 17-footer and aged centre pin, which we all know is essential at these ancient ponds.

"Indeed it was suggested that Trevor's slow start with the crucians was down to the fact that he was using a very impressive and shiny fixed spool engine. Our fish are sensitive to such things, the Manager said.

"Trevor had chosen 'Jim's Swim' while Jim had chosen 'Pete's', where his masterly skill, snared the crucian of the day, a 'pound-and-a-halfer' and several others.

"On display was the finest of fine tackle, with floats dotted down to pin pricks. Baits were many and marvellous: worms dunked in groundbait, fragments of flake within blobs of a lovingly moulded mixture of mashed bread and rice - 'cupping' Trevor called it - maggots, tares and exotic pellets. The Manager confided to Hugh that sweetcorn wasn't much of a bait there and was immediately proved wrong by two crucians coming to the net on half a grain within five minutes.

"Lunch came soon enough, with Trevor's Kelly kettle singing merrily and pluming smoke. There was plenty of joshing and reminiscing, mugs of tea and generous slices of Hugh's Sue's Victoria sponge. After cake, it was back to work, with varying degrees of success, though that didn't matter a jot. Catching fish was almost unimportant on a day of companionship and memories.

The Saxon Ponds

"There's a storm on the way", said a slightly worried Jim. "Look at the radar picture." Bright colours were approaching on his screen and there was an ominous continuous rumbling over towards our hilltop town. We packed in something of a hurry, deciding that carbon rods and lightning don't mix well, and gathered in the barn to finish the rest of Hugh's sponge. The rain drummed on the roof in tropical fury, but we were dry and snug.

"Then, as in Beethoven's 'Pastoral', the sagging black clouds opened up to sunshine. The thunderous roll of timpani gave way to gentle strings and oboes and we packed and paid our farewells in summer warmth. As Hugh wrote later: 'That was as good as a day's fishing ever gets, so thank you all for the excellent company ... and we even caught some beautiful fish.'"

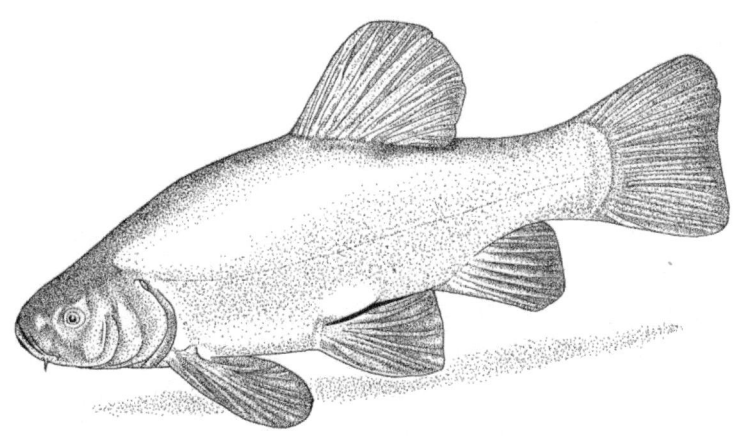

The Saxon Ponds

August 8th, 2021: The Day We Drained the Lower Pond

"This was a day that could well have turned out to be a disappointment, even a disaster, but was in the event a triumph – good fun, too! Even the weather was on our side. The overnight rain had relented and returned only after we were safely home.

"Thanks to the efforts of the weed-clearers during the previous week, there was a fairly open area immediately upstream of the sluice and a channel linking that to the island. The mounds of raked weed were impressive, a mix of broad-leafed pondweed, hornwort and algae. We also lifted boards one by one during the week so that by 'the day' only two were left, each 8" deep.

"There was plenty of weed left, though, and I worried that fish would get trapped in it when the water level dropped. Because of this possible problem, we began by letting the water out gradually, to give the fish a chance to follow the flow into the open patches. As an extra precaution, we had 'gleaners', who got into the mud and weed with hand nets and buckets to save any fish they could find.

"At the sluice we had two strong fish-farming handnets, which side-by-side covered the opening. At first, every few minutes these were lifted, the board replaced so as not to lose fish downstream, and any fish caught transferred to the tubs on the dam. We quickly found that the nets' mesh clogged and slowed down the rate of draining. The fish were anyway reluctant to follow the current through the sluice, preferring to swim against it and stay within the pond.

"So we changed our technique. Steve and Nigel were able to walk upstream along the cleared channel, through silt at least knee-deep, sometimes more, to net the fish. We had 'sweepers' at the sluice to rescue any fish that escaped past Steve and Nigel. The 'gleaners' too were able to struggle through weed and silt into the pond and rescued many fish that way. Weed drags and a prong were helpful.

"The fish were put in the filled tubs on the dam and sorted. There were plenty of hand-sized crucians, with some rather larger, including one of well over 1lb. The one tench in the pond, put in at

The Saxon Ponds

about 8", had grown to a respectable couple of pounds. About 25 bigger crucians and the tench were transferred to the upper pond. We found a surprising number of small roach and perch. There were some crayfish and, interestingly, a number of tiny water scorpions, indicators of good water quality like the water stick-insect Jim had found in the upper pond a month earlier.

"The crucians, except for the biggest, must have been young fish bred in the pond, not the result of previous stocking. The lack of big crucians suggests to me that the sanctuaries had not worked well enough to withstand the prolonged cormorant attacks of the winter before last. Presumably the crucians we rescued yesterday had been too small then to attract the attention of the darn birds.

"The success of the day was down to the enthusiasm and hard work of many people, and I'll try to list all of them. During the previous week, Cole and Garry, who couldn't be there for the draining, worked hard at the very dirty job of weed-clearing, as did Nick, Steve, Nigel and Rob. It would all have been so much more difficult on 'the day' but for their efforts. Every evening we had two workers there.

"Dave the contractor and his three helpers made things a lot easier for us. They pumped water into the tubs so that we didn't have the labour of doing it with buckets and a chain gang and were towers of strength in gathering fish at the sluice. The tractor and trailer made light work of getting stuff back to the yard and having water on tap cleaned things off nicely.

"Rob and David made very welcome guest appearances to great effect. As we've come to expect, 'the Dabblers' were amazing in their efforts: Chris, Duncan, Nick, Steve, Nigel and Rob put in nearly five hours of hard labour. And last but not least, the two boys – members for the future perhaps – Finley and Harry – who enjoyed the mud like everyone else and found short boots no problem!

"My musings, to finish with. The pond is due to be dredged next month – the machines are booked for 6th September. Paths, new sluice, bridges, boat houses, etc., with all appear in due course. I'll

The Saxon Ponds

keep you all up to date as things go on. I hope that all the activity will keep the black plague away over the winter but we'll take our own precautions too for the upper pond. Next April, when the lower pond has filled and has had time to build up some invertebrates, we'll net the upper pond and move fish down so that you can fish both next season.

"Thank you all for your efforts and if I've missed anyone out, please put it down to my forgetfulness, not lack of gratitude.

"P.S. Would you believe it! Rob found two tailless crucians amongst the weed. Presumably the result of cormorant damage when very young. They were otherwise fit and healthy fish with the terrible wounds well healed. They should be recognisable!"

October 3rd, 2021: Manager's Musings

"The dredging is now finished. More than 800 dumper loads of silt have been moved to the dumping area or bund in the lower lying area of the top field. At about 40 tons per load, that's a lot of weight, though much of it is water of course. There will be 8' of water in several places when the pond is refilled, much deeper than it has ever been, so the fish will have plenty of room.

"Now, it looks like a scene from a WW1 battlefield but I know how quickly nature restores things and by next summer all will look superb, I'm sure. Then we can re-stock as we wish, though first we need to see our fish in the upper pond safely through the winter. There is much to look forward to."

June 16th, 2022: Cole's Opening Day

"Although I'm generally up and moving by 7:30am, getting up at 3am seems increasingly outside the rabbit-proof fence. This said, everything being prepped on the eve, left only putting heat under the coffee pot, putting the resulting contents into the flask and nabbing breakfast from the fridge…bumping along the stony track, there is enough light to see a full-grown hare startled by the side-

The Saxon Ponds

lights, dashing hither and yon in the insane way of hares. I pause, watch, forget to reach for the camera. Never before seen one here.

"It's hard to decide whether I prefer the camera's determined attempts to take the picture it thinks I want, or the phone's entirely reasonable pictures of the actual scene. I take a few snaps with both, loiter in the cool sepia-toned dawn, watch wraiths of mist glide across the pond and then, in near silence, slink around to the Semley bank. I pitch quietly, then with the light carp rod, fish for opening-day tench.

"After 30 minutes, I carefully miss a bite. After another 30 I strike optimistically at the first tench of the season. This turns out to be a small perch. Makes sense. Five minutes later comes tinca minor. Heh. Then tinca median 40oz or so, then tinca major at 54oz. The air is still cool enough that the water feels warm, so I decide it's breakfast time. There are two hard-boiled eggs, two (technically) sandwiches, hunks of olive-bread crammed with a selection of smoked salamis and cheese slices, plus fresh Cairo coffee (made with a teaspoon of ground cardamom in with the coffee. Really rather good...).

"The day crept from grey to green, a breeze blew the last spectres across the pond into my face, I was half-expecting them to develop teeth and shriek. I glared balefully at a raven on the top-most dead branch of a tree opposite, which I suspected of eyeing up my sandwich.

"Then the half-light was gone, the sun was up, Nick arrived, Terry arrived, the tench appeared to have left. I succumbed to the lure of the rolling crucians, got the light rod from the car and caught crucians on pinches of bread including one fine, but underfed looking fish. Pete came by on his rounds. I swapped banks to the shady side, my first pitch now in blazing sun.

"Jim turned up and ambled about getting into fishing mode, not before spotting a mass migration of toadlets amongst the comfrey and on closer inspection there were dozens of them, inching away from the pond.

The Saxon Ponds

"Nick, after a fine catch of crucians and roach did the same, heading for lunch and then the Bristol Avon. Terry caught three crayfish amongst scattered perches, roaches and crucians. Jim settled in my original pitch and started to extract tench that I'd neglected. Terry, having exhausted the crayfish, went on. I was lured by the prospect of a few more unplanned hours, so nipped of to the high-road shop for cold ginger beer, sandwiches and lemon cake, to sustain the inner angler. I returned, edged the chair into semi-shade, fed-and-watered. Martin turned up and set about setting up. There were more crucians, the bankside temperature hit 27°C, a couple more tinca minors, some fine roaches, perches and a quantity of Arcadian musing. At about six bell, I hit some kind of barrier; heat/sufficient fish/too old for 3am alarm-calls. One of those..."

September 17th, 2022: Manager's Musings

"The upper pond has fished well this season, and there's still another month to go before the crucians stop feeding, as long as the weather stays mild. It's often very productive in October, though not too many people fish it then. The roach should be coming into top condition and there's always a chance of a late tench or two, if you can keep them out of the lilies!

"The perch have been a bit of an enigma. Usually, small perch can be a pain because of their numbers, but that hasn't been the case in the upper pond for some reason. There's been no real evidence of bigger perch being there, although that may be because no-one has targeted them.

"Over the season we've moved over 600 fish to the lower pond, mostly small crucians but with a mix of roach and perch as well. At the last fish-in/social there was some evidence that this is helping the fish in the upper pond to put on weight. Thanks to all of you who joined our fish-ins. I hope that you enjoyed them as much as I did.

"No-one has fished the lower pond, though we have three tasty-looking swims available on the wild north bank. Access has been

The Saxon Ponds

improved. You can get in via the 'Wiltshire gate' about halfway down the fence. That takes you directly to the top swim of the three, with deep water under the rod tip and water lilies and bushes as features.

"I shall be away on holiday for the last week in September. When I get back, it'll be time to think about protecting our fish from cormorants again. I'll send out a separate email to arrange that. I'd like to get that done in October, before the water lilies die back and make the fish more vulnerable."

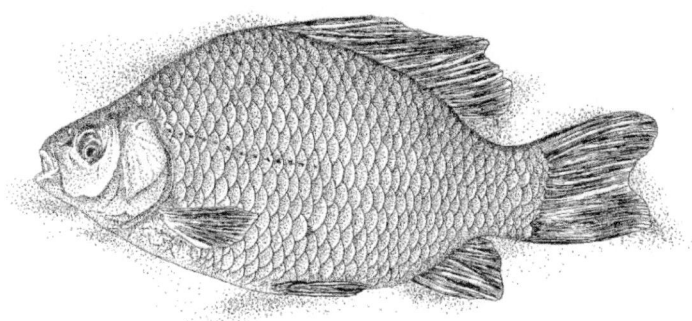

The Saxon Ponds

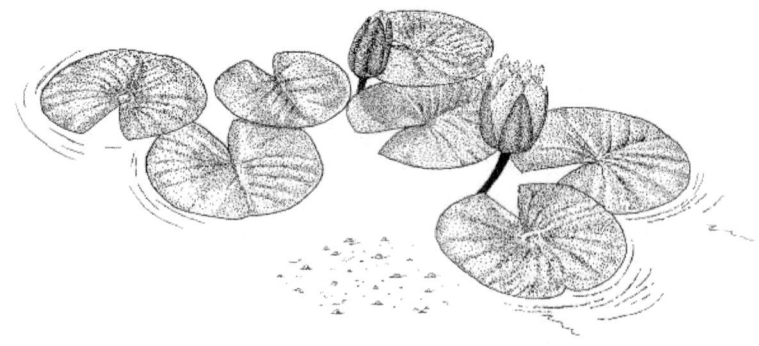

The Saxon Ponds

EPILOGUE

The Future

Looking at the lower pond now, two years after its completion, it is difficult to recapture the mixture of consternation, excitement and admiration that its dredging caused. Perhaps now it does justify the description that the lawyers insisted on in drawing up my licence to organise the fishing here: it is indeed more 'lake' than 'pond'.

Horace Chapman's island has gone, scooped up by a massive machine along with thousands of tons of silt. It and its surrounding brickwork are now unidentifiable debris in the heaps of spoil slowly drying in a low spot in the pasture bordering the upper pond. The lake looks much bigger than it ever did, every square yard of its

The Saxon Ponds

three-quarters of an acre. It is far deeper now, probably eight feet instead of the three to four feet that I remember from the old days.

The sluice and concrete block dam that caused us so many problems in the past have been replaced by a new structure of tremendous solidity. "That's not going anywhere," said Dave, the contractor, with a smile of satisfaction.

An extensive timber jetty has been built in one corner, with a mooring place for an elegant rowing boat. I occasionally stand on its edge and look down into the deep water, following the line of the oak piling, looking for the first signs of life in the spring and imagining great perch lurking beneath the woodwork. Toadpoles abound in May, around the jetty and along this dam bank, as indeed they do in the still-to-be-developed upper pond.

At the inflow end of the lake, stylish sandstone steps allow swimmers to clamber from the clear-brown water. One bank is revetted with substantial coconut-fibre rolls, behind which wildflower seeds have been sown to complement the white iris beds by the sluice and steps. A turf path winds along this south bank.

The north bank has sensitively been left wild and it is here that we have three swims. There we can fish unobtrusively, invisible from the house and lawns that overlook the lake. The view across the water from these swims is garden-like, though time will remedy this, as the willow pollards transferred from their original position along the dam grow their yellow branches and the bankside vegetation grows abundantly, as it always does. Nature abhors a vacuum.

Beyond the bank is a wildflower meadow, some ten yards wide and nearly the length of the lake, a riot of colour by the end of last summer. Attractive estate fencing in black metal separates the lake area from the parkland beyond, where isolated broadleaf trees grace grassland dotted with sheep.

Already, wildlife is recolonising the lake: moorhens and duck are plentiful; a mallards' nest half-concealed by newly sprouting sedge has seven eggs in it; the clouds of non-biting midges promise abundant food for swallows and fish.

The Saxon Ponds

The great alders that have for generations overshadowed the water on this bank are still there. Willows, too, and native white water lilies remain as familiar friends.

Eventually, new estate fencing will replace the stock-proof wire that still skirts this side of the lake. I hope that anglers' access will not be forgotten, though the future for fishermen here is as yet unclear.

I am reminded that Horace Chapman, too, built his ponds to be an extension to his garden, as is now the case with the new owner. It was only time and neglect that turned them into the delightful wilderness that Bob and I found on our first exploration 50 years ago.

***

The upper pond remains a 'pond'. As I write this, in the late spring of 2023, I know that it is as shallow as it ever was, even shallower. Where the water enters the pond, the stands of reedmace are denser than ever, impeding the passage of the clinging silt that the winter floods have brought in despite the new, deep and extensive trap in the field upstream. Left unattended, the pond will eventually become dry land again, just as it has done in the past.

Even in its decline, though, the pond remains a delight, surrounded by sheep-filled pasture, with the wood on the slope overlooking it all. Further up the hill, a small herd of black and cream alpacas replaces sheep, a sign of changing times. But the clock of the medieval church on the hill still marks the fishing hours with its chimes; bell-ringers practise their tunes and add music to the many charms of this little-frequented place.

Wildlife still gathers to its epicentre. Owls keep company with late anglers and the bats flicker overhead as the light diminishes, preying on the myriads of midges whose countless larvae are food for our fish. Sometimes a late angler will see the luminescence of a glow-worm and mistake it for a lost 'Starlight' float. Sometimes he will be intrigued by a bizarre hawk moth caterpillar. A barn owl

The Saxon Ponds

quartering the pasture for voles and mice gives us all a thrill of recognition, a white companion in the gloom.

Dragonflies make sunny summer days more colourful and hobbies prey on them, flashing across the surface almost too quickly to see. Duck, moorhens, little grebe and herons enjoy the plenty that the pond provides. Here, if anywhere, you can enjoy the rare sight of a kingfisher perched brilliantly on your rod, hear it whistle in flight and recognise its feathery splash as it dives for tiny fish.

In the water, living alongside our crucians, tench, perch and roach, plus of course Moby Dick, are brook lampreys, huge freshwater mussels and countless invertebrates. Rare water stick insects and freshwater scorpions, the predatory larvae of water beetles, dragonflies and damselflies lead their hidden lives in their own savage jungle.

Sedges and flag iris greet the spring and the white blooms of the water lilies follow. The grasses and buttercups crowd the fishermen's paths and regret the scythe and slasher.

Fishermen's swims discreetly hide amidst reeds and sedges, with wood chippings ensuring pleasant sitting. The bubblings of crucians, tench and roach promise good sport, and the water lily pads twitch as great fish move from place to place. There is always the hope of a two-pound crucian or roach, and the lure of tench nearing four pounds.

***

Yet all this beauty and wonder will fall victim to time unless man intervenes to desilt the pond and restore the crumbling dam. Soil brought down by the brook will accumulate until water becomes dry land. Leaks will hasten the process. The pond will become dry land. Then, other life forms will replace aquatic ones.

Here is the dilemma. Ironically, restoration and maintenance with modern machinery destroy what they seek to perpetuate. They wipe the slate clean: the millions of living things that depend upon the pond die beneath the heaps of desiccating silt. Those that can, seek

The Saxon Ponds

another home: the lower lake will become a refuge for the fortunate few.

The methods of the past – hand maintenance, little and often; partial draining and drying; labour-intensive hand dredging, pruning and path-making – are not for this modern age. Rolf's slow, cheap-labour management is a thing of a remote past, environmentally preferable though it was; as remote now as the building of the Pyramids or the Great Wall of China or digging canals by hand. Now, we destroy to renew.

Without sacrifice, though, these ancient pools in their precious landscape will not survive. The legend of the phoenix comes to mind: re-birth will have to come from destruction.

This is indeed what the future holds for the upper pond. In a year or two's time, attention will turn to replacing the dam and deepening the water. Perhaps the ' upper pond' will turn into the 'upper lake'. A new cycle of life will begin. Rolf, Ralph, Chapman and Rolfe will be forgotten but for the few who read this book.

The Saxon Ponds

The Saxon Ponds

Printed in Great Britain
by Amazon